"*Ant* Faith doesn't want to get married.

She told *Mamm* she's not 'mantically interested in—"

"Look!" Faith interrupted, taking her nephew by the hand and distracting Hunter. "Here comes your *daed*. He's been searching for you."

When his father walked through the throng of wedding guests, he didn't scold the boy. "One of the challenges of being a *daed* is knowing when to show grace and when to stand firm," he explained.

"Being a *daed* is a weighty responsibility, for sure," Hunter said. "But I'm told it's one of life's greatest blessings."

The words stung Faith. Until then she hadn't realized her affection for him. Hadn't realized she secretly imagined walking out with him. Imagined they would grow from business partners and friends to much more.

But they were just silly daydreams. Hunter had made it clear he wouldn't court anyone he didn't intend to marry. And now she knew he could never marry her.

So why did she still wish this was their wedding celebration?

Carrie Lighte lives in Massachusetts, where her neighbors include several Mennonite farming families. She loves traveling and first learned about Amish culture when she visited Lancaster County, Pennsylvania, as a young girl. When she isn't writing or reading, she enjoys baking bread, playing word games and hiking, but her all-time favorite activity is bodyboarding with her loved ones when the surf's up at Coast Guard Beach on Cape Cod.

Books by Carrie Lighte

Love Inspired

Amish Country Courtships

Amish Triplets for Christmas
Anna's Forgotten Fiancé
An Amish Holiday Wedding

An Amish Holiday Wedding

Carrie Lighte

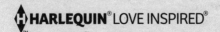

Recycling programs for this product may not exist in your area.

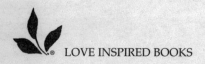

® LOVE INSPIRED BOOKS

ISBN-13: 978-1-335-42835-6

An Amish Holiday Wedding

www.Harlequin.com

Printed in U.S.A.

And he said unto me,
My grace is sufficient for thee: for my strength
is made perfect in weakness. Most gladly
therefore will I rather glory in my infirmities,
that the power of Christ may rest upon me.
—*2 Corinthians* 12:9

For those who are strong enough
to share their vulnerabilities.

With continued thanks to my agent,
Pam Hopkins, and my editor, Shana Asaro.

Chapter One

Faith Yoder secured her shawl tightly around her shoulders, climbed onto the front seat of the bicycle built for two and began pedaling toward Main Street. It wasn't quite five o'clock in the morning and her brothers hadn't yet risen to do the milking. Her headlight cast a weak glow, barely illuminating the empty lane in front of her. The rest of Willow Creek, Pennsylvania, was still asleep and the November moon was her only companion.

Or almost her only companion. As she made a wide turn onto the primary stretch of road leading into town, she spied a lone figure lumbering beneath the streetlamp a few yards ahead of her.

"Watch out!" she warned as her downhill momentum propelled her closer.

The man lifted his head but didn't move from

her path, so she quickly swerved onto the shoulder to avoid hitting him. Her front wheel wobbled off the road and into the shallow ditch, causing her to lose her balance.

"My *oier*!" she shouted and jumped clear of the heavy bicycle, which clattered on its side. The cargo she'd been carrying in a crate strapped onto the backseat—two dozen eggs—smashed against the pavement. "My *oier* are ruined and now my cupcakes will be, too!"

"You ought to be as concerned about hitting pedestrians as you are about making cupcakes," the man replied in *Pennsilfaanisch Deitsch* as he hobbled to where she was searching the ground for any unbroken eggs.

"I *didn't* hit you, so you can quit that limping," she contended and peered at him under the dim circle of light cast by the streetlamp.

Although the young man's hair was mostly hidden by his hat, a few dark brown curls sprang from beneath the brim. He wore no beard, which meant he'd never been married. He was average height, but his shoulders seemed unusually broad beneath his wool coat. She didn't recognize him as being from Willow Creek. Most Amish women in their district wouldn't have argued with a stranger on a deserted road in the wee hours of the morning, but Faith Yoder wasn't most Amish women. Having grown up with six brothers, she knew how to hold her own.

"If you're so worried about getting hit," she continued, "you could exercise common sense and walk on the side of the road, not in the middle of the lane."

The man seemed at a temporary loss for words. He gave her a once-over before replying, "It seems strange you're lecturing me on common sense, when you're the one riding a tandem bicycle pell-mell through the pitch-dark with a basket of *oier* strapped to the backseat. You might consider getting a headlamp."

"For one thing, it's not pitch-dark—there's a full moon out. And for another, I *have* a headlamp," Faith retorted, setting her bike upright and extending the kickstand.

But noting the sickly glow waning from the light on her handlebars, she recognized she probably bore the responsibility for their near-collision. Chagrinned, she added, "It does seem I need to replace my battery. I hadn't noticed. I travel this road so often I probably could make the trip blindfolded. My name is Faith Yoder. What's yours?"

She couldn't tell whether it was a smile or a grimace that flickered across the man's face. "I'm Hunter Schwartz, Ruth Graber's great-nephew."

Hunter Schwartz, of course. Faith had heard

Hunter was bringing his mother from their home in Parkersville, Indiana, to care for Ruth. The elderly woman had broken her ankle and severely sprained her wrist after falling from a stepladder in the little cannery she owned across the street from Faith's bakery.

Faith should have recognized Hunter from his childhood visits. If it hadn't been so dark, she undoubtedly would have spotted the cleft in his chin and remembered his earnest brown eyes. Coupled with a valiant personality, his boyish brawniness had caused many of the young *meed* to dream of being courted by him the autumn he was sixteen.

"I'm sorry," Faith apologized. "I didn't recognize you. It's been a long time."

If Faith remembered correctly, the last time he'd been in Willow Creek was the year his great-uncle died. After the funeral, Hunter stayed for several months to fix Ruth's roof and help with other household repairs. It was during harvest season, when many of the *leit*, or Amish people in the district, were tending their crops, and Hunter frequently helped out on the Yoders' farm, as well as attended singings and other social events with Faith's brothers. The following year, he'd gotten a full-time job in Indiana working for the *Englisch*, who limited his holiday breaks. From then on, Ruth said it made more sense for her to visit Hunter's family in Indiana than for them to travel to Willow Creek, and he hadn't been back since.

"*Jah*, about eight years," he answered. "I didn't recognize you either. You've, er, you've really grown."

She'd really grown? Faith knew what that meant, and she smoothed her skirt over her stomach. There was no denying she'd put on weight since she was a scrawny, flat-as-a-washboard tomboy, but she rather appreciated the womanly curves she once wondered if she'd ever develop. Well, she mostly appreciated them, anyway. She'd lost all but fifteen of the pounds she'd gained after Lawrence Miller broke off their courtship. Now she was down to the weight she was while she and Lawrence were courting. She didn't consider herself fat, but she wasn't thin by any standard. Still, she thought it was impolite for Hunter to draw attention to her size; he used to be so well mannered. But, reminding herself vanity was a sin, she shrugged off his observation.

"I suppose it was my fault I nearly ran into you. I'm grateful it's only my *oier* and not your legs that are cracked," she conceded amicably.

Hunter again looked taken aback, almost as if she'd insulted him instead of apologized. He paused before saying, "I'm sorry about your *oier*, too, but at least they were only intended for dessert instead of for breakfast. Most people can do without cupcakes, but not without a meal."

Now Faith couldn't deny feeling insulted. Who did Hunter think he was, assuming she was making the cupcakes as a mere indulgence for herself, just because she was a bit...a bit *round*?

"For your information, I own a bakery in town and the *oier* were for cupcakes I need to make for an *Englisch* customer," she sputtered as she mounted her bike. "The customer's *daed* is turning seventy-five and this special birthday treat is as important to their family as your breakfast apparently is to you, so I'd better be on my way to remedy the situation. *Mach's gut*, Hunter. Enjoy your morning meal."

Without another word, she sped away as quickly as she could pedal.

Hunter rubbed his jaw, watching Faith disappear into the dark. His bewilderment about her hasty departure temporarily distracted him from the pain coursing through his lower back and legs. Had his jest about her bike riding offended her? Or was it that she expected him to have known she was a business owner? If anything, he figured *he* should have been insulted by *her* remarks. Was she trying to be funny, chastising him not to limp? And what about her remark about being grateful his legs weren't cracked? Considering his physical condition, that was nothing short of cruel.

But as he trudged back toward his aunt's home, Hunter realized that however unnerving Faith's comments were, she must have made them in complete ignorance. His aunt undoubtedly told the *leit* in Willow Creek about the accident that took his father's life, but she wouldn't have necessarily told them about Hunter's ongoing recovery from his own injuries, especially since he concealed his pain from everyone, even his family members. Besides, from what Hunter recalled, Faith Yoder simply didn't have a cruel bone in her body. She was tough, yes. Outspoken, definitely. But Hunter remembered that as a young girl, she went out of her way to demonstrate compassion and generosity, especially toward anyone who was mistreated, ill or otherwise suffering.

Granted, Faith was no longer a young girl. It had been too dark to get more than a glimpse of her, but he'd noticed the sharp angles of her girlish face had been replaced with a becoming, feminine softness. Gone was the rash of freckles splashed across her nose; her skin appeared as lustrous and unblemished as the moon. Hunter wouldn't have believed the same scrappy girl he'd known from his youth had blossomed into the stately young woman he encountered on the road that morning if she hadn't told him her name: Faith Yoder. Yoder—that meant she was still unmarried, although Hunter assumed she was being courted, perhaps was even betrothed.

Imagining Faith's suitors reminded him of Justine, the woman he'd walked out with in Indiana. She was devastated when Hunter ended their relationship after his accident a little more than a year ago. It pained him to cause her heartache, but breaking up was in her best interest: Hunter wouldn't seriously court a woman he didn't intend to marry, and he wouldn't marry a woman if he couldn't be a good provider for their family. After all, the accident cost him his job at the *Englisch* RV factory and it had severely limited his mobility. At the time Hunter broke up with Justine, there was no telling whether he'd even be able to walk again.

Eventually, Justine accepted another man's offer of courtship, and now she'd be getting married in two weeks. It was exactly what Hunter prayed would happen for her, but he was still relieved he wouldn't be in Indiana to attend her wedding. While he no longer cared for Justine the way he once did, witnessing her getting married would have emphasized how much his life had changed since they were courting. Shivering, he forced thoughts of the past from his mind.

The frosty air intensified the ache clenching his lower spine. He stopped and waited for it to pass. The long van ride from Parkersville had wreaked havoc on his body. Walking into town didn't help much, but it was better than lying in bed, waiting for the minutes to pass and the pain to subside.

"Guder mariye," he greeted his mother when he returned, startled to see her out of bed. For years, her rheumatoid arthritis manifested itself in periods of extreme fatigue and sore, swollen joints, and ever since Hunter's father died, her flare-ups were more frequent and intense. "You're up early."

"Jah, and your *Ant* Ruth is awake, too," his mother replied. "I'm fixing her something to eat. She was asking after you, since she was asleep when we arrived last night. Would you keep her company while I make breakfast?"

Hunter tentatively approached the parlor where his aunt was reclining on the sofa with her leg propped on a stool. Her skin was pale and she wore a white cast on her foot, as well as a sling on her arm, but her eyes were lively.

"There he is, my favorite nephew!" she squealed. Despite his pain, Hunter chuckled at their old joke; he was Ruth's *only* nephew. After giving her a careful embrace, he asked, "How are you feeling, *Ant* Ruth?"

"I'm madder than a wet hen!" she exclaimed. "You probably know better than anyone how frustrating it is to be confined to bed when you're used to being out and about."

Hunter clenched his jaw. "That I do."

"But it's worth it if it means I get to see you and your *mamm's* faces again," Ruth said, her voice softening. "I wish I could see your *daed's* face again, too."

Hunter shared the same wish. The last time he'd seen his father's face was the evening of the accident, some fifteen months ago. They were returning home from work when a truck driver lost his brakes, sideswiped their buggy and rammed into the wall of an overpass, where he perished in the fiery crash. Hunter and his father were trapped beneath their mangled, overturned buggy, unable to help him or themselves.

"Hunter, if *Gott* spares your life, promise you'll take *gut* care of your *mamm*," his father pleaded while he lay dying. After Hunter agreed, his father whispered, "Two of my greatest blessings in this lifetime were being a husband to your *mamm* and a *daed* to you. I couldn't have asked the Lord for a better wife or *suh*."

"Nor I for a better *daed*," Hunter echoed before passing out. By the time he was cognizant enough to speak again, Hunter learned he was in the hospital and his father had already been buried for three days.

Remembering, Hunter shuddered and shifted in his chair. To his relief, his aunt changed the subject.

"Mmm, that smells good. What is your *mamm* making for breakfast?"

"*Oier*, I think," Hunter guessed. Then he launched into a narrative of his roadside encounter with Faith.

"Ach!" Ruth exclaimed. "What a fiasco! You must collect *oier* from the henhouse and deliver them to Faith after breakfast. She'll need them to fill her customers' orders."

"I'm the last person she wants to see again today," Hunter protested.

More to the point, he didn't want to see *her* again today. In fact, he didn't wish to see—or to be seen—by anyone in Willow Creek just yet. The questions about his circumstances would come soon enough; he'd rather field them after he recovered from the tiresome journey.

"Nonsense! Take the buggy if you'd like, but it's the right thing to do, even if Faith was at fault. She'll be so glad to see you coming she might even treat you to one of her *appenditlich* cream-filled doughnuts. The trip will be worth your while."

"Okay," Hunter agreed. He knew better than to argue with his aunt once she'd made up her mind, but he'd made up his mind, too. He'd drop the eggs off, but he wasn't going to hang around Faith's bakery eating doughnuts, no matter how delicious Ruth claimed they were.

Of all days to have an egg mishap, Faith was dismayed it happened on a Saturday, the busiest day of the week and the same day she had a special order to fill. When she arrived at the bakery, she surveyed the glass display case, taking inventory.

The honey bars would stay moist through Monday. There were plenty of fresh whoopee pies and molasses cookies, but she'd have to move the cinnamon rolls to the day-old shelf. She had intended to start a few batches of her renowned cream-filled doughnuts before the bakery opened at seven, but now she wouldn't have enough eggs. When her only employee, Pearl Hostetler, arrived, she'd ask her to whisk over to the mercantile, which didn't open until eight thirty, to purchase more. Meanwhile, the egg shortage would put them behind schedule on all their baking for the day.

Faith sighed. First things first. She set about

mixing yeast with hot water. Although she preferred baking more elaborate goodies, several of her *Englisch* customers depended on her for homemade bread. Every purchase counted if she was going to meet her financial goal by the first of the year, which was only a month and a half away.

That was the deadline the *Englisch* landlord required for the down payment on next year's lease. In addition to the small storefront and kitchen, Faith would also rent the one-room apartment above the shop, since the current tenant was moving out. He was the third resident to leave in four years, and with each turnover, there had been a three-or four-month delay before a new resident moved in. Disgruntled by the gap in revenue, the landlord was adamant that from now on, the apartment and building space were to be a package deal. Faith either had to rent both or lose the bakery to Seth Helmuth, who wanted to set up a leather shop in the prime location downstairs and use the upstairs apartment for storage and supplies. But Faith had first dibs, and although the down payment amount was more than she had saved, she was arduously working to earn the total sum.

"Won't you be lonely, living all by yourself?" Pearl asked when she discovered Faith would be moving into the apartment.

Living alone wasn't something most Amish women voluntarily chose to do, and as someone who dearly missed her three children who moved out of state, Pearl couldn't fathom why the opportunity might appeal to Faith.

"I won't have time to be lonely," Faith responded. "I'll wake up and *kumme* right down here, where I'll have the privilege of working with you and visiting our neighbors and serving our customers. I'll spend the better part of Sundays and holidays with my family and with the church. The only difference is I won't have to ride my brothers' old hand-me-down tandem bicycle to get here each day."

Faith's sister-in-law Henrietta was even more dismayed about Faith's decision.

"You can't allow her to separate herself from the family like this," she once told Faith's oldest brother, Reuben.

"The *Ordnung* doesn't forbid it, so neither do I," Reuben replied. "Faith is a thoughtful person. I trust she prayed about this decision and is aware of the challenges."

As the eldest son, Reuben became the head of the family when their *daed* died five years earlier, since their *mamm* had passed away five years before then. Reuben and Henrietta lived in the large Yoder farmhouse with their three young sons, Faith and four of her five other brothers. The fifth brother, Noah, lived with his wife, Lovina, and their children in a small adjoining *daadi haus*. Faith knew she'd always have a place and purpose within her family, but given how cramped their dwelling was, she couldn't understand why Henrietta objected to her moving.

"If you live alone, you'll appear uncooperative or proud. You've already got one significant reason a man wouldn't wish to marry you—do you want to make it even more difficult to find a mate?" her sister-in-law asked her.

While Faith knew Henrietta had her best interests at heart, her words stung. The "significant reason" a man wouldn't wish to marry her was Faith's most intimate secret, something only family members knew. Well, only family members and Lawrence Miller. Faith felt compelled to confide in her former suitor after he asked her to marry him two years ago.

She vigorously kneaded a lump of dough as she recalled the afternoon she disclosed her secret to him. She'd been so nervous she hadn't eaten for two days, and when she finally worked up the courage to tell him, she was uncharacteristically tearful.

"There's a possibility I might not be able to bear *kinner*," she confessed, chewing her lip to keep herself from weeping.

The color drained from Lawrence's long, thin face as he slowly shook his head. That's what Faith remembered most clearly—his shaking his head without saying a word.

She was too modest to explain that the year she turned seventeen, she had surgery to remove dozens of cysts from her ovaries. The cysts were benign, but the doctor warned the surgery caused scarring that could result in infertility. At the time, her relief over not having the kind of cancer that claimed her mother's life outweighed any concern Faith had about not bearing children. She hadn't fully appreciated the repercussions of the surgery until she and Lawrence began walking out and planning a future together.

"I know how upsetting this must be to hear," she consoled him. "But if it turns out I can't become, well, you know… We might consider adopting—"

She may as well have suggested flying an *Englisch* rocket to the moon to retrieve a child there for how preposterous Lawrence claimed her idea was. Adoption took too much time, he said, and it was too costly to adopt one child, much less the six or eight he was hoping to have.

"The doctor said there's a *possibility* I won't be able to have *kinner*," Faith emphasized in between the sobs she no longer tried to stifle. "It's only a *possibility*."

"I'm sorry, Faith, but that's not good enough for me," he said.

She knew he meant *she* wasn't good enough for him. She was damaged. Scarred. Less than a woman. She understood then that she'd probably never marry—at least, not until she was much older, or unless a widower with children of his own sought to court her. And since she wouldn't marry, there was no sense courting, either. But Faith didn't mind because it meant she'd never have to tell any man her secret ever again. The rejection and the shame of disclosing her condition were more than she could bear a second time.

She clapped the flour from her hands as if to banish the memory of Lawrence from her mind. Regardless of what Henrietta or anyone else said, she didn't need a *mate* to take care of her. With God's grace, she'd take care of herself just fine. As for living alone, she was looking forward to it.

For the moment, she had six dozen lemon cupcakes with lemon buttercream frosting to prepare for the *Englischer* who'd pick them up at eleven o'clock. She started mixing the ingredients, using every egg that wasn't required for the egg wash for the bread. She'd have to forgo making doughnuts until later, but her customers would just have to settle for something else.

We don't always get what we want, she thought as she mixed the batter into a smooth, creamy texture. *But we can make the most of the options we have.*

Which was exactly what she intended to do herself. No matter what anyone thought about her decision to live alone, Faith was determined not to lose the bakery. A few cracked eggs or critical remarks weren't going to keep her from accomplishing her goal. Nor was a future without a husband going to keep her from being happy.

During breakfast, Hunter's aunt asked if he'd assist her with a significant undertaking.

"Of course I'll help you, *Ant* Ruth. That's why I'm here. I'm happy to make house repairs and tend to the yard and stable. Do you need me to take you to your doctor's appointments, as well?"

"*Jah*, I have appointments coming up soon. But what I really need you to do is oversee my shop. It's been closed for the past week, and Thanksgiving and *Grischtdaag* are just around the bend. They're my busiest seasons."

Hunter took a large bite of biscuit so his mouth was too full to respond. His uncle owned a furniture restoration business, with his main workshop at home and a smaller storefront in town. After he died, Ruth converted the space in town into a cannery, where she sold jams, relishes, fruits and chow chow. Hunter knew nothing about canning, and he didn't particularly care to learn.

As if reading his mind, Ruth explained, "You wouldn't be expected to do the canning. I've put up plenty of jars for now, and harvest season is over. If the shelves run low, your *mamm* has agreed to help with the canning, although she'll have to use store-bought produce for the ingredients, which is what I sometimes do in the winter."

"You want me to serve customers?" Hunter questioned. "I wouldn't be able to distinguish pickled beets from raspberry preserves!"

"*Neh.* My employee, Ivy Sutter, waits on customers. She knows everything there is to know about the products. But she has a special way of learning, so when she's ringing up purchases, she needs supervision—and protection. She's such an innocent *maedel.* Our regular customers are fine people, *Englisch* and Amish alike, but I'm concerned some of the tourists might take advantage or make demands."

Hunter set down his fork. He was familiar with his aunt's compassion for anyone who struggled with a difference of ability or who didn't fit in as well as others did. But Ruth was gifted; she had a way with people. He didn't. At least, he didn't anymore. Most days, his pain was so intense it took all of his resolve not to snarl at his own mother. How would he tolerate demanding customers or keep his patience with a girl who had learning difficulties?

"You wouldn't just be supervising Ivy. You'd also restock the shelves and keep the books. Of course, I'd pay you fairly," Ruth concluded.

"He wouldn't think of accepting payment, would you, Hunter?" his mother, Iris, interjected.

Hunter's ears felt inflamed. He knew it was a sin to be prideful, but his aunt's offer of a salary wounded his ego—primarily because he was in such desperate need of an income. It had been so long since he'd had full-time employment, he forgot what it felt like to receive an honest day's wage. Since his accident, he'd taken as many odd jobs as he could get, but they were few and far in between. The *leit* in his district helped with a significant portion of his hospital bills, but his rehabilitation was ongoing. In fact, he'd prematurely quit physical therapy because he knew they could no longer afford the sessions *and* pay for his mother's medical costs. He didn't want to keep imposing on the church, especially since others' needs seemed greater than his own.

Most humiliating of all, right before they left for Willow Creek, he'd received a notice from the bank stating they were on the brink of losing the house if they were delinquent with another mortgage payment. To the Amish, making a payment late was considered almost akin to stealing, since it denied the payee their fair due on time. While the payments were very small, Hunter still had difficulty scraping together enough to cover the mortgage. He shielded his mother from their financial woes, but he was so overwhelmed he was tempted to accept a lawyer's offer to sue the trucking company that employed the driver who hit them. Thankfully, the temptation left him almost as soon as it struck: it was unthinkable for the Amish to engage in a lawsuit for financial gain.

Swallowing the last of his coffee, Hunter decided although he might not be able to provide for a wife and he was floundering in caring for his mother, the least he could do was manage his aunt's shop without accepting a cent for it. He'd always had an interest in bookkeeping; perhaps the experience would afford him new skills he could use in Indiana.

"We're family and we're here to help, *Ant* Ruth," he finally stated. "Provided there's absolutely no more talk of payment, I'll be glad to oversee your cannery."

Yet as he hitched his horse to the post in town, he was anything but glad. Rather, his legs were so sore and stiff they felt like two planks nailed to his hips. He tottered down Main Street with a basket of eggs, hoping he didn't appear as conspicuous as he felt.

Stopping beneath the simply carved sign that read Yoder's Bakery, Hunter noticed a smaller cardboard sign propped in the window. "Early morning delivery person URGENTLY needed. November 27–December 24. Willow Creek to Piney Hill. Inquire within," it said. He wondered how "early" was early. Could he make the deliveries and still return to Willow Creek in time to open the cannery? Would Faith even consider him for the job, given their interaction that morning?

Hunter squinted through the spotless glass window. The bakery contained five or six small tables with chairs. Beyond the cozy dining space was a pastry case and behind that Faith was stacking bread on a shelf. Hunter noticed what had been too dim to see earlier: the fiery red hair of her youth had faded to a richer, subdued shade of auburn.

"Do you see something in there you think

you'd like?" a woman behind him asked. "Everything we make is excellent."

Embarrassed, Hunter turned and stuttered, "You—you work there?"

"I do. My name is Pearl Hostetler. But wait—aren't you Hunter, Ruth's nephew?" the tall, thin, silver-haired woman asked.

"I am," he answered sheepishly. "It's *gut* to see you again."

"It's *wunderbaar* to see you, Hunter," Pearl said, placing her hand on his arm. "Ruth told me about your *daed*. I was very sorry to hear what happened."

"Denki." He coughed, surprised by the emotion Pearl's sincere sympathy elicited. He extended the basket of eggs. "I brought these for Faith. Hers broke this morning when she was cycling into town. Also, I'm… I'm interested in hearing more about the delivery job."

Hunter hoped Pearl would simply receive the basket and provide him details about the job, but she pushed the door open and announced, "Look who's here, Faith. Hunter brought you *oier* and he wants to be your deliveryman, as well!"

Noticing Faith's eyes narrow, Hunter didn't wish to appear too eager. He clarified, "I'd like to hear more about the job, that is."

"It's pretty straightforward," Faith replied,

brushing her hands against her apron. "I need someone unfailingly dependable to deliver my baked goods to an *Englisch* booth at the Piney Hill Festival between seven and seven thirty every morning, Monday through Saturday. The festival begins in less than two weeks, on the day after Thanksgiving, and runs until the day before *Grischtdaag*. The delivery person would have to commit for the duration of the festival in order to make it worth my while to rent booth space."

Mentally calculating the distance between the bakery and Piney Hill, Hunter was certain he could complete the deliveries, return the horse and buggy to his aunt's home and walk to town with a good fifteen minutes to spare before the cannery opened at nine o'clock. And when Pearl blurted out the sum he'd earn for each delivery, Hunter was confident the arrangement was an answer to his prayers.

Looking Faith in the eye, he said, "Beginning Monday, I'll be managing Ruth's shop from nine until five o'clock, but I'd be available in the early morning to make deliveries for the duration of the festival."

Faith nodded slowly. "*Jah*, I'd appreciate that. The job is yours," she confirmed. She paused as a mischievous grin crossed her face. "But I do hope you're more careful about where you steer than you are about where you walk. My sales are very important to me."

"Your sales will be fine, provided you bake better than you bike," Hunter retorted, giving her an equally rascally smirk before setting the eggs on a table and exiting the store.

As he stepped into the brightening day, he realized Ruth was right: the trip had been worth his while. Being a part-time deliveryman for Faith Yoder might not have been his first choice for employment, but it was a steady, paying job, and that was all that mattered to him.

Chapter Two

After the door closed behind Hunter, Pearl dramatically clasped her hands together. "Ach! What a relief that is! I was beginning to think we weren't going to be able to sell our goods at the festival."

Hosted by a neighboring town right off the main interstate, the Piney Hill Christmas Festival was an enormous, commercial *Englisch* endeavor attracting thousands of passersby shopping for Christmas. Part of its appeal was the "Christmas Kingdom"—an elaborate prefabricated "Santa's Workshop" where children could have their photos taken with Santa. The bishop didn't prohibit the Amish *leit* from selling their goods at the festival, as long as they only rented space at booths hosted by the *Englisch* and didn't staff the booths themselves.

"Jah," Faith said, tentatively optimistic. "Al-

though there's no guarantee we'll sell enough at the festival to make the down payment, without it, we wouldn't have stood a chance."

"It's a *gut* thing Hunter is in town again, both for Ruth and for us," Pearl gushed, hanging her shawl on a peg inside the hall leading to the kitchen. "Hasn't he grown into a fine, strapping young man?"

Although Hunter's mature physique hadn't escaped Faith's notice, she didn't know quite what to make of his personality. He definitely seemed more personable just now than he'd been on the road earlier that morning, and bringing her eggs was a nice gesture, but that might have been at Ruth's urging. Before Faith could respond, the phone rang and Pearl grabbed the receiver. "Yoder's Bakery, how may I help you?"

Landlines and electricity weren't allowed in Amish homes, but the *Ordnung* permitted them to be used for business purposes in their district, provided the buildings were owned by the *Englisch*. The bakery utilized both electricity and a phone, but neither service would be continued in the overhead apartment once the current tenant moved out, making it permissible for Faith to live there.

After hanging up, Pearl waved a slip of paper. "Another pie order for Thanksgiving! Two apple and one sawdust. If this keeps up, you'll have to start turning down orders."

"Not if I want to keep the bakery, I won't. I'll bake every night until midnight if I have to."

Although one of her chores growing up included baking for her family, Faith hadn't always enjoyed the responsibility. But while she was recovering from surgery, she began experimenting with dessert recipes. She soon discovered that even among the Amish she possessed an unusual talent for making goodies, and she reveled in the process of creating savory treats. That autumn, she made cakes for her second-oldest brother Noah's wedding to Lovina that were so scrumptious several guests requested she bake for their special occasions, too. Faith's business was born.

Sharing a kitchen with Henrietta proved to be impractical for both of them, however, so eventually Faith rented her current space. The bakery was the one good thing that resulted from her surgery, and she had no intention of letting it go without doing everything she could to raise the income for the down payment for her lease. So, when an *Englisch* customer called to say he couldn't pick up his large, unpaid order by the time the bakery closed at five, Faith continued to make pies to freeze for Thanksgiving until he showed up. It was six thirty by the time she finally locked the door behind her.

A frosty gust nearly blew her outer bonnet off her head as she pedaled uphill in the dark toward the big farmhouse. She meant to purchase a new battery at the mercantile during her dinner break, but she'd been so busy she didn't stop for an afternoon meal. Ravenous, she hoped her family hadn't worried about her when she missed supper.

"There you are," Henrietta said when Faith entered the kitchen. Her cheek was smudged with flour and she was jostling her youngest son on her hip. Utensils and ingredients were spread in disarray across the table. "Didn't you remember you were going to help make the bread for dinner tomorrow?"

The following day was their Sunday to host church worship services and they would need to serve a light dinner to everyone in attendance. Henrietta usually provided the traditional after-church meal of bread with "church peanut butter," homemade bologna, cheese, pickles and pickled beets. An assortment of desserts were supplied by other women in the district.

"Ach! I forgot," admitted Faith.

"You mustn't put earning money before the needs of the church," Henrietta scolded.

Faith hung her head. She wouldn't have

stayed so late waiting for the customer if she'd remembered she promised to help bake bread after supper. Still, the fact that she'd forgotten indicated her priorities were on her business, not on the church.

"I'm sorry," she earnestly apologized. "I'll make the bread as soon as I've had something to eat."

"Something to eat? Your *ant* works in a bakery all day and she expects us to believe she hasn't had anything to eat," Henrietta cooed to the infant, who drooled when she tickled the fold of skin beneath his chin. "Do you believe that? Do you?"

Unsure whether her sister-in-law was joking or not, Faith ignored her comment. She opened the icebox and removed a bowl of chicken casserole to eat cold, along with a serving of homemade applesauce.

"Did I tell you my sister is visiting for Thanksgiving?" Henrietta asked while Faith devoured her supper. "My *mamm* and *daed* can't make the long journey, but I haven't seen Willa for so long that I pleaded with her to *kumme* anyway. She'll have to travel alone, which is difficult for her. She's not as…*strong-minded* as you are, but she misses me, too, so she's willing to make the effort. It will be *wunderbaar* to have another woman in the house, someone I can talk to."

Maybe she was overly tired, but Henrietta's comments nettled Faith and she had to work to temper her response. "That's nice. I'm sure we'll make room for her somewhere."

Then she washed, dried and put away her dish and utensils before rolling up her sleeves to prepare the dough. It would be midnight before she finished baking after all.

Although Hunter felt his lower back seize up as he lifted Ruth into the buggy on Sunday, he met the challenge without a word of complaint. The Amish only missed church in cases of severe illness or extreme circumstances, and according to Ruth, her injuries weren't going to keep her from worshipping on the Sabbath.

"Do you remember the way to the Yoders' farm?" she asked. "It's their turn to host."

Hunter hadn't forgotten. He'd spent many Sunday afternoons fishing in the creek behind their property with Noah and Mason Yoder when he was a youth. As the horse pulled their buggy over the familiar hills and alongside the pastures and farmlands on the rural end of Willow Creek, he was flooded with remembrances of more carefree times.

After church service, men whose names he'd

forgotten but whose faces were etched in his memory affably welcomed Hunter to the men's dinner table. By then, his legs were throbbing from sitting on the cold, hard benches in the drafty barn the Yoders used for a gathering room. He ate even quicker than the other men, who were all aware someone else was waiting for a turn at the table and hurried to vacate their places. Hunter wanted to return to Ruth's home and warm himself in front of the woodstove, but he didn't see his aunt and mother anywhere. Undoubtedly, Ruth was chatting with friends while his mother helped the other women clear tables and clean dishes.

Figuring if he couldn't warm his aching legs, he could at least stretch them, he slipped away from the men conversing in small clusters and awkwardly navigated the uneven terrain leading to the creek a few acres behind the Yoders' house.

He didn't notice until too late that a woman was already there, leaning against a willow, pitching stones sidearm into the current. He couldn't turn around without being rude and he couldn't keep moving without drawing attention to his unsteady gait, so he came to an abrupt standstill.

"*Guder nammidaag*, Hunter," she called when she noticed him, dropping the stones.

It was Faith. Hunter had no option but to continue in her direction and hope she didn't notice his unusual stride. He didn't want her to doubt his abilities and regret hiring him.

"Guder nammidaag," he replied and motioned toward the water. "The creek is shallower than I remember. I suppose everything probably seemed bigger when I was a *kind*."

"We had a dry summer, so it's been running low," she acknowledged. "Do you really still remember the creek?"

"How could I forget?" Hunter asked as he positioned himself next to her. "The year I was twelve, Noah, Mason and I tried to build a footbridge over it and it collapsed. Don't you remember? You were there, too."

A smile capered from Faith's lips up to her eyes, and for an instant her expression reminded Hunter of the spunky young girl who used to tag along on her brothers' adventures. "You boys sent me across the bridge first to test whether it would hold," she recalled.

Hunter reminisced, *"Jah*, but you were only a little wisp of a thing, so of course it withstood your weight. I don't know what we were thinking, for the three of us boys to join you on it, with none of us knowing how to swim. It was a *gut* thing your *daed* heard our cries and ran to give us his hand."

Now a shadow troubled Faith's countenance. "Sometimes I wish my *daed* would still *kumme* running to give me his hand, even though I'm no longer a *kind* and it's been five years since he died," she lamented.

Hunter hadn't meant to stir up sad memories. "I'm sorry about your *daed*. I have fond memories of him," he said. He was quiet before adding, "My own *daed* died a little over a year ago, so I understand why you miss yours."

"I'm sorry for your loss, too, Hunter," Faith murmured, her hazel eyes welling with empathy. "I should have said as much yesterday. My brothers were especially grieved to hear about the accident. Ruth mentioned you were hurt in it as well, but I'm grateful to see *Gott* answered all our prayers by healing you."

Not wishing to admit he wasn't fully recovered, Hunter blew on his fingers and then changed the subject. "A lot has changed since we were *kinner*. Who would have expected little Faith Yoder would grow up to own a bakery?"

A furrow momentarily creased Faith's brow before she straightened her posture and asked, "And what about you? Do you still work at the RV factory?"

Pushing his hat up, Hunter massaged his forehead. The crick in his spine seemed to be traveling upward, giving him a headache. He didn't want to be dishonest with Faith, but he was concerned if people knew about his job loss, he might become the object of gossip. Or worse, the object of pity.

"I—I—" he stuttered.

His sentence was cut short by Mason calling out, "Faith! Hunter! We've been looking for you!"

Faith's brother traipsed down the hill in their direction, and Lawrence Miller ambled a few paces behind. They were followed by two young women. Hunter sensed the questions he'd been dreading had only just begun.

As she watched her peers approach, Faith felt uncharacteristically peevish.

Ordinarily, she relished the time she spent chatting with the other women during Sabbath dinner cleanup, but today Lawrence's fiancée, Penelope Lapp—an eighteen-year-old deacon's daughter who lived in a neighboring town—was visiting her relatives in Willow Creek. After church, Faith overheard Penelope fawning over Henrietta's infant, claiming she hoped God would bless her with a baby by this time next year.

Although Faith no longer felt any romantic attachment to Lawrence, it distressed her to be reminded of why they'd broken up. She escaped to the creek to gather her composure, only to be discovered by Hunter, who pointed out what a "little wisp of a thing" she used to be and made her sentimental by calling to mind a long-forgotten memory of her departed father.

If all that weren't unsettling enough, now she was going to have to exchange pleasantries with Lawrence!

"Hunter, how *gut* it is to see you," Mason said, clapping him on the back.

Lawrence did the same and Hunter responded in kind.

"Please meet Katie Fisher," Faith's brother said. "She's the schoolteacher here."

"And this is Penelope Lapp," Lawrence stated. "My intended."

"Your intended?" Hunter repeated.

"Don't sound so surprised," Lawrence ribbed him. "I'm twenty-two, almost twenty-three. It's past time for me to marry and start a family."

Faith winced, supposing if it weren't for the time he lost courting her, Lawrence wouldn't feel his marriage and family plans were behind schedule.

"How about you, Hunter?" Penelope asked. "Are you betrothed or walking out with someone?"

"Neh," was all he said.

"Neh? That's a surprise," Lawrence replied.

To Penelope, he explained, "Hunter lived here for a while when he was sixteen and he was so sought after, he had his choice of *meed*. He could have courted anyone he wanted."

Faith's irritation was becoming more difficult to suppress—it sounded as if Lawrence were describing horses at an auction, not young women.

"Did you want him to court you, Faith?" Penelope asked.

"I was only thirteen!" Faith exclaimed. "Despite what some people may think, not every *maedel's* sole dream is to get married as soon as she possibly can."

She was appalled by Penelope's nerve. Even if Faith had developed a crush on someone as a schoolgirl, it wasn't something she'd discuss, especially not in front of male acquaintances. Courtships and romance among the Amish tended to be private matters.

"He didn't court or even favor anyone, if I recall," Lawrence said. "He claimed he didn't believe in courting unless he intended to marry, and since he was only sixteen and lived in Indiana, there was no point in walking out with anyone here. He was probably the only person who actually attended our singings just for the singing."

Penelope sniggled but Katie asserted, "*I* attended singings in my district primarily for the singing when I was a youth. There's nothing wrong with that."

Faith smiled at the stout, dark-haired woman. She always appreciated Katie's forthright manner, and she was glad Mason was walking out with her. When Faith glanced at Hunter, she noticed he was shifting his weight from foot to foot, as if embarrassed by the conversation. She couldn't blame him and she quickly switched topics.

"Speaking of youth, Hunter and I were just talking about how you boys used to spend time down here at the creek," she said to Mason. "Do you remember the footbridge?"

"*Jah*, of course." Mason regaled the others with the anecdote about their footbridge disaster and subsequent submersion in the creek.

"After your *daed* pulled us out, he promised if you finished the fieldwork early the following week, he'd help us build a sturdier bridge," Hunter recalled.

"*Jah*, and you were so excited that after working all day for Ruth, you'd come and help us every evening in the fields and on Saturday, as well," Mason reminisced, shaking his head. "My *daed* frequently commented about what a strong, dedicated worker you were. I often had to ask *Gott* to forgive my envy."

"He's still strong—look at those shoulders," Lawrence observed, lightly punching Hunter's arm.

Faith wasn't certain if she imagined it, but Hunter's face seemed to go gray. Was it modesty or the cold wind that caused him to set his jaw like that? Although as a boy, he was as congenial as could be, there was something stilted about his posture now that gave him an air of aloofness. Ordinarily, Faith would have been put off by an unsociable demeanor, but she sensed Hunter was uncomfortable with the attention, and she wanted to spare him further uneasiness.

"The bridge is still standing," she informed Hunter. "This past summer I brought my nephew down to the water so he could cross it."

Hunter visibly relaxed his shoulders. "I'm not surprised," he said, looking directly at Faith as he smiled. "Your *daed* made sure it was durable."

"I'd like to see it," Penelope suggested. "Why don't the men lead the way?"

Faith had never taken Lawrence to the bridge before, and she didn't want him visiting it now. The bridge belonged to another part of her life; it belonged to her dad and brothers and nephews—and even to Hunter. But not to Lawrence. "I really ought to return to the house—" she started to say.

"There's no need to hurry back," insisted Penelope. "If you're hungry, there will still be leftovers in another hour. And it's not as if you need to dash to the evening singing to meet a suitor, is it?"

Faith huffed. She never mentioned wanting to eat, and she didn't appreciate Penelope's digging for information about whether she was being courted. "Actually, my concern is that I ought to be helping clean up."

"But who knows when I'll be back here again?" Penelope sounded like a wheedling child. "Please, Faith?"

"Alright," Faith agreed, "*kumme* along." She had no idea why it was so important to Penelope to see the footbridge, but she gave in since the young woman was a guest in their district. As a member of the host family, it was up to Faith to be especially hospitable to her. But that didn't mean she was going to let the men take the lead.

Although Faith courteously accommodated Penelope's request, as she pivoted toward the woods Hunter noticed the spark in her eyes. What put it there? Why did she suddenly say she needed to get back to the house? Was it really that she wanted to help clean up, or did Faith have a suitor waiting after church for her? Hunter didn't know why the possibility caused him to experience a twinge of disappointment now, when only yesterday he assumed she was being courted. But perhaps that wasn't the reason she wanted to leave at all. Maybe Faith was simply tiring of Penelope's intrusive inquiries.

Hunter sure was. He gladly would have returned to the house, too, but the only thing he wanted to do less than hike along the creek was to explain why he didn't want to hike along the creek. He intended to avoid discussing his injuries as long as he could. After all, what would Lawrence say once he knew Hunter developed such broad shoulders from months of turning the wheels of a wheelchair and hoisting himself along the parallel bars at the clinic? Would Mason think Hunter was less of a hard worker when he found out he'd lost his job because he wasn't mobile enough to meet the assembly quota at the RV factory? Would it suddenly dawn on all of them why he was no longer "sought after" as a bachelor? What might Faith—not just as his employer, but as a woman near his age—think of him then?

It wasn't that Hunter believed any of them would be unsympathetic if they found out about his injuries; it was that he didn't want their sympathy in the first place. He worked too hard at recovering to have to answer personal questions about his condition from the likes of Penelope Lapp. So he bit his lip and tried to match his stride to Mason's and Katie's, while Faith marched up ahead and Penelope and Lawrence lagged behind.

"How long will you be visiting Willow Creek?" Katie questioned conversationally.

"Until my *ant's* leg heals, probably sometime after the first of the year. I'm managing her store until she's better." Hunter pushed a branch out of his way, holding it to the side so it wouldn't spring back and hit Penelope.

"What do you do for employment at home?" Penelope questioned.

"He works in an RV factory, isn't that right?" Lawrence replied before Hunter had a chance to answer. "You must have accrued a lot of time off to take such a long leave. That's one *gut* thing about working for the *Englisch*. It's not like a farmer's work, which is never done."

While Hunter contemplated how best to respond, Penelope swatted at Lawrence with the end of her shawl. "I've heard it said that it's a farmer's *wife's* work that is never done," she taunted.

"That, too," Lawrence allowed.

"Business owners don't exactly sit around twiddling their thumbs, and Katie has her hands full as a schoolteacher, too," Faith countered over her shoulder. Hunter chortled inwardly in appreciation of her feisty tone. She was never one to let her brothers claim their work was more important or difficult than anyone else's, including hers, when they were kids.

"*Jah*, that's probably true," Penelope concurred. "Oh! Speaking of business owners, I almost forgot. Lawrence and I want you to make the cakes for our wedding, don't we, Lawrence?"

"*Jah*, if she's willing."

"Of course I'm willing, but please give me your exact order ten days in advance. I know Lawrence prefers everything to be just so, and I wouldn't want to disappoint him," Faith said without slowing or turning to face them. Did Hunter detect a note of sarcasm in her reply?

"I will," Penelope agreed happily. "Hunter, you must attend our wedding, too. All of the *leit* from Lawrence's church are invited. We'll match you up with a—"

"There's the bridge," Faith interrupted, and Hunter was thankful she'd saved him from embarrassment once again. She scampered down the rocky embankment, and the others followed.

Each step seemed to jar Hunter's hip bones against their sockets as he descended the slope. The small bridge was weathered and a few boards were missing, but it rose in a functional arc above the shallow current, just as he'd remembered.

"It's as good as new," Mason jested, confidently crossing it to the other side. He held out his hand for Katie to join him.

Katie stalled reluctantly. "I don't know… I might be too heavy for a *kinner's* bridge."

"Don't you trust my workmanship?" Mason teased, so she darted across the planks.

Penelope took her turn, and then Lawrence stepped onto the structure. "You call this durable?" he gibed, stomping on the bridge with the heel of his boot. "This board here feels a little loose."

After Lawrence crossed, Hunter waited for Faith, who seemed to be dillydallying. "Ladies first," he uttered patiently.

Faith hesitated before placing one foot onto the bridge. As she lifted her back foot from the shore, the waterlogged board beneath her front foot gave way.

From the parallel embankment, Katie shrieked, "Help her!"

It happened so suddenly and his joints were so stiff, Hunter wasn't able to spring forward quickly enough to prevent Faith from falling. Her front leg wedged through the crack into the creek while her upper torso lurched forward onto the bridge.

Mason and Lawrence raced down the opposite bank while Hunter bolted into the icy current from his side of the water. With one foot dangling in the creek, Faith was using her dry, bent leg and her arms to try to crawl onto the bridge.

"Are you hurt?" Mason asked.

"I'm *stuck*!" she yelped, red-faced. "Stop pulling me! You're making it worse."

"I've got her," Hunter said authoritatively. "I'll lift her up so you can free her leg. Be careful. Here, Faith, lean back against me."

From behind, he gently wrapped his arms around her waist and clasped her to his chest until Lawrence and Mason eased her leg from between the planks. Then he carried her to the embankment. Her stocking was torn and her leg was scraped from her ankle to her knee, but it didn't appear to be seriously injured.

Kneeling before her, Hunter hesitated. He feared his legs would lock up on him, but he offered, "If it hurts your ankle to walk on it, I can carry you back to the house."

"Neh," she snapped and what seemed like a look of disgust clouded her face. He didn't blame her; he might as well have pushed her into the creek for as slowly as he'd moved to prevent her from falling in.

Then she quietly added, *"Denki,* but my foot is fine. It's just very cold, so I'm going to hurry up ahead."

Katie, who had waded over to be sure Faith

was alright, said, "My feet are wet and cold, too, so I'll go with you." She linked her arm through Faith's for support and they scuttled away.

Stranded on the opposite bank without a bridge to cross, Penelope called, "What about me? Lawrence, help!" until Lawrence waded across the water, hefted her to his shoulder as easily as a sack of grain and waded back, setting her down next to Mason and Hunter.

The four of them walked in silence the rest of the way, too chilled to speak. In fact, until Katie mentioned her feet were wet, Hunter hadn't realized his legs were, too. The icy water had made them so numb that for once he wasn't aware they'd ever been hurt at all. Wishing the same could be said of his self-esteem, Hunter kept his chin tucked to his chest as he tramped against the wind.

Chapter Three

On Sunday night, Faith rose so many times to don her prayer *kapp* and kneel beside her bed that she feared she'd wake her two nephews, ages three and five, who slept on the other side of the divider in the tiny room she shared with them. Each time she finished praying, she was certain she'd thought her final uncharitable thought, but another one would come to mind as soon as she slid back under the quilt and she'd have to ask the Lord to forgive her all over again.

Much of her resentment was directed at Lawrence, whom she blamed for her clumsy plunge into the creek. If he hadn't deliberately trampled over the bridge like a big ox, the board wouldn't have broken when it was her turn to cross. She was equally piqued by Penelope's constant chatter and references to her upcoming wedding.

Faith understood the young woman was barely eighteen, but it seemed she could have exercised a bit more discretion.

Yet oddly, it was Hunter's conduct that ruffled her most. Rationally, she knew he was being helpful, but she was utterly mortified when he wrapped his arms around her midsection and held her above the water. Not to mention how embarrassed she was by the pained expression on his face right before he offered to carry her home. He couldn't have appeared more daunted if he'd volunteered to shoulder a dairy cow!

She admitted she was overweight, but she wasn't *that* overweight. Wasn't Hunter supposed to possess extraordinary strength, anyway? Wasn't that what Mason and Lawrence claimed? She remembered his youthful vitality, too, just like she remembered how popular he was. But what good did either of those qualities do him now, if he couldn't be gracious enough to overlook the fact she was no longer "a little wisp of a thing"? Not that she wanted his assistance, but he didn't have to pull such a face when he offered it—especially in front of Lawrence and his skinny fiancée, Penelope.

Faith socked her pillow. With the exception of the afternoon she confided her secret to Lawrence, she'd never felt so unfeminine and humiliated as she'd felt that afternoon. By the time she drifted to sleep, she wasn't certain whether her leg ached from falling through the bridge or from kneeling so long, praying for God to forgive her pride and anger.

When she awoke on Monday, her indignation had faded, but as she bicycled through the dark, her leg burned with each painful rotation of the pedals. Feeling cranky, she hoped she'd have a few minutes alone before Pearl arrived. Usually, the older woman didn't come in until seven thirty or eight, but this week she planned to work longer hours to help fill the Thanksgiving pie orders.

Faith sighed. Thanksgiving was ten days away and they were behind schedule as it was. They'd received so many orders that Faith resorted to limiting the number of fresh-baked pies she'd sell during the half week before the holiday. Instead, she offered customers the option of buying unbaked, frozen pies, which they could pick up anytime. Many *Englischers* said they'd be glad to experience the fragrant aroma of "homemade" pies baking in their ovens. Some brought in their own pie plates, and Faith inferred they might intend to take credit for making the pies themselves, but she didn't mind one bit; each order brought her closer to making her down payment.

But exactly how much closer was she? The

surge in orders was generating more income, but since she was also spending more on ingredients and paying Pearl for extended hours, Faith wasn't sure how the figures would balance out. Bookkeeping wasn't her strength, but she planned to review her financial records as soon as things slowed down in the bakery.

"Guder mariye," Pearl cheerfully greeted Faith. "You're limping! What happened to your leg? Were you romping through the woods with those darling nephews of yours again? You dote on them. You'll make a fine mother someday—"

"It's nothing," Faith cut in. She was edgy enough without being reminded she probably *wouldn't* make a fine mother someday. "You're here even earlier than I am. Did you start a pot of *kaffi?*"

"I just put it on."

They took turns making and rolling pie dough and peeling and slicing apples until it was time to flip the sign on the door to Open.

"Guess who's up bright and early this morning?" Pearl chirped, returning from the task. "Hunter Schwartz. I spotted him in the shop."

Her cheeks burning at the mention of Hunter's name, Faith only mumbled, "Hmm."

"The cannery doesn't open until nine. He must be an especially hard worker."

First Pearl called him a fine, strapping young

man and now she was praising his industrious-
ness. Faith knew the older woman well enough
to suspect her comments were a prelude to
matchmaking.

"Jah," Faith carefully concurred. "Diligence
was always one of Hunter's admirable attri-
butes, even when we were *kinner.*" Then, so
Pearl wouldn't read any personal interest into
Faith's admission, she added, "That's one of the
reasons I didn't hesitate to hire him."

"We should extend a personal invitation for
him to join us for his afternoon meal, the way
Ivy and Ruth always do. You could go over there
before the customers start arriving and—"

Now Faith felt positive Pearl was laying
the groundwork for a match between her and
Hunter. *"Neh!"* she refused more adamantly
than she intended.

Pearl put her hand to her throat as if wounded.
"Oh," she apologized meekly. "I just thought it
would be a neighborly thing to do."

Faith realized she may have misinterpreted
Pearl's intentions and regretted her decision hurt
Pearl's feelings, but she didn't back down. "It's
a lovely thought, Pearl. But we're so busy filling orders I don't foresee myself taking proper
dinner breaks. It wouldn't be polite for me to
personally invite him and then not join all of
you once he got here."

"*Neh*, of course not, I understand," Pearl said. "Work comes first."

"I didn't mean that," Faith clarified. "I only meant..."

The bell jangled on the door and one of the *Englisch* regulars stopped in for his morning coffee and honey bar. Faith was relieved she didn't have to confess the real reasons she couldn't possibly sit down and eat dinner with Hunter Schwartz. For one thing, even though he was already well aware of the size of her waist, she didn't want him to know how much she ate and judge her for it. For another, there was something about seeing him again as an adult that made her doubt she could swallow two bites in front of him. The feeling wasn't merely the awkwardness over broken eggs or broken bridges, nor was it necessarily an unpleasant sensation, but it was unsettling all the same. Once Faith became accustomed to working with him, perhaps she'd feel different. For now, she hoped she wouldn't see much of Hunter until after Thanksgiving, when he began making deliveries. Perhaps by then, she'd even lose a couple of pounds.

Hunter wiped his palms against his trousers. On Saturday he'd mopped the floor, and he'd come into the cannery early this morning to restock the shelves so that everything was exactly where it should be. Rather, everything except one very important person: Ivy. It was ten minutes before nine o'clock. The shop opened at nine on weekdays, and Ivy was nowhere to be seen.

Hunter was afraid this might happen. Ivy lived alone with her grandfather, Mervin Sutter, who introduced Ivy to Hunter and Iris after church on Sunday. The blonde, petite, sixteen-year-old girl wouldn't look Hunter in the eye as she mumbled a barely audible greeting. He attributed her shyness to his own appearance, assuming she was intimidated because he was twice her size. Also, his pants were dripping from walking into the creek and he was shaking with cold. To her, he probably looked like a crazed bear, which was a bit how he felt at that particular moment.

Glancing through the window toward the bakery, he wondered how Faith's leg was this morning. He knew from experience pain had a way of getting worse as the day wore on. As he uttered a quick prayer this wouldn't be the case for Faith, he caught sight of her approaching a table toward the front of her shop. She disposed of a napkin and paper cup and scrubbed the table in swift circles with a cloth. To his surprise, when she was done she lifted her hand in acknowledgment. Pleased she seemed to have put his shortcomings during yesterday's incident behind her, he waved back.

Then he realized she wasn't waving to him, but to Ivy, who was passing on the sidewalk in front of the cannery. She pulled the door open just as the clock began to chime on the hour.

"Ruth Graber turns the sign to Open at nine o'clock," Ivy stated in a monotone.

Hunter was startled speechless by her greeting. Then he recalled Ruth advising him that habits were very important to Ivy and he mustn't disrupt her routine.

"Of course, *denki* for the reminder, Ivy," he said as he flipped the sign on the door.

For the rest of the morning, Ivy didn't say a word unless asked. But she led the customers to any item they requested and she could quote the jars' contents and prices by heart. However, Hunter quickly discovered that while her recitation skills were excellent, Ivy had no ability to add or multiply figures. So, he used the cash register to create receipts while she bagged the customers' purchases.

Virtually all of the customers were *Englischers*, but at midmorning, a slightly built, bespectacled Amish man, Joseph Schrock, paid a visit to introduce himself. Joseph's father, Daniel Schrock, owned Schrock's Shop, which featured Amish-made crafts and goods that were especially appealing to tourists, and the store turned a healthy profit.

"It's *gut* to meet another businessman," Joseph said. "Sometimes I catch grief because I'm not a carpenter or a farmer, but I knew from the time I was a *kind* I had a head for figures, not a body for a farm. *Gott* gives us all different talents, right?"

"*Jah*," Hunter agreed, although he wasn't sure if Joseph's comment made him feel better or worse about not being able to do the physical labor he'd been accustomed to doing. What if his physical strength was his only God-given gift? What if he didn't have a "head for figures"?

He didn't have time to dwell on the thought, though, because customers were lining up. Soon, Ivy declared, "It's quarter to one. Ruth Graber and I take our dinner break with Faith Yoder and Pearl Hostetler at one o'clock. Ruth Graber turns the sign to Closed."

Hunter didn't mind if Ivy went to Faith's bakery for her dinner break, but he had no intention of going with her. During the working day on Main Street, his association with Faith was strictly professional, not social. "You've done such a *gut* job teaching me how to serve customers, Ivy, that I'll keep the shop open and stay here while you take your break."

The girl's face puckered in confusion. "You won't eat with us?"

"I'll eat my dinner now in the back room. If any customers *kumme* in and you need help, call me. I'll be done before one o'clock," Hunter assured her.

In the sterile back room where Ruth did her canning, Hunter leaned against a stool. Standing all morning caused his hips and lower spine to burn with pain, but if he'd been sitting all morning, he would have claimed the same discomfort. The fact was, there was little that didn't cause his back and legs to hurt and even less that helped them to feel better.

He listened for customers arriving as he downed his cold mincemeat pie. After church, Henrietta Yoder sent a pie home with them, saying Faith made the pie especially for Ruth the evening before, once she finished baking bread for the church meal. Hunter, his aunt and his mother enjoyed it for supper, and he was pleased there were leftovers he could bring to work for dinner. If the rest of Faith's baking was as good as her pie, Hunter figured it was no wonder her business was flourishing.

He returned to the main room with four minutes to spare. The door was left open and Ivy was gone.

"Ach!" he said aloud. "She must have gone to Faith's already."

Yet it troubled him that she'd left the door ajar. Also, she was so time-conscious that it seemed unlikely she would have left before the clock chimed. However reluctant he was to face Faith again after his ineptness at the creek, Hunter wouldn't be satisfied until he made certain Ivy was at the bakery. He put on his coat and hat and crossed the street.

"Guder nammidaag!" Pearl exclaimed when he stepped inside, where a tantalizing aroma filled the air. "Faith, look who's joining us for his dinner break."

"Oh?" Faith's neutral response was difficult to interpret as she bent to slide a tray of apple fry pies into the display case.

"Actually, I already ate my dinner," Hunter explained. "I'm here to check on Ivy. She left without letting me know she was going."

Faith abruptly popped up from behind the counter, her eyes wide. "Ivy's not here. She never steps foot in the door until the clock strikes. How long has she been missing?"

"Missing? I don't think she's *missing*," Hunter faltered as a wave of panic washed over him. "She's just not at the shop, that's all."

* * *

Noticing Hunter's ashen complexion, Faith felt almost as much concern for him as she did for Ivy.

"Don't worry, we'll find her," Faith promised. "When exactly was she last in the store?"

Hunter stammered, "She—she was just there fifteen minutes ago. It was quarter to one. I told her I'd eat my dinner in the back room and when I was finished she could *kumme* here to take her dinner break with you."

Faith immediately knew what the problem was, but she didn't have time to explain it to Hunter. She glanced at Pearl, who was already tying her winter bonnet beneath her chin.

"I'll check the other Main Street shops for her, but meanwhile you'd better get to the pond," Pearl advised. "She has a fifteen-minute head start."

Grabbing her shawl, Faith asked Hunter if he'd brought his buggy into town.

"*Neh.* I walked."

"Follow me, then," she urged and led him through the kitchen and out the back door. She wheeled her tandem bicycle away from the wall it was leaning against.

"You can take the backseat, I'll steer," she instructed. Although the pond was situated right down the hill from his aunt's house, Hunter was so dazed Faith wasn't sure he'd remember where to turn off the main road.

"We're going to ride the bike?" Hunter asked. He seemed to be moving in slow motion and Faith wondered what was wrong with him. Was he in shock?

"*Jah*, now hop on," Faith ordered, hoping her no-nonsense attitude would bring him to his senses. "I'll tell you more as we ride, but for now I need you to pedal as hard as you can."

They wobbled a bit as they started down the secondary road running parallel to busy Main Street, but after three or four rotations, Faith felt the bicycle surge forward and suddenly they were sailing. She immediately recognized Hunter's reputation for stamina was well earned: the heavy bike never glided so briskly when Faith rode it alone. If she weren't so distraught about Ivy, she might have enjoyed the rush of nippy November air against her cheeks as they cruised along together.

"Where are we going?" Hunter shouted.

"Wheeler's Bridge," Faith spoke loudly over her shoulder.

The covered bridge spanned the far end of Willow Creek, which wound its way through much of the farmland in the area, including the Yoders' property. As a small, single-lane structure, the bridge was mostly used by Amish buggies or by tourists taking photos. It was situated just before the point where the current pooled into a deep and sizable pond.

Faith noticed an immediate lag in their speed as Hunter gasped. "Do you think Ivy might have jumped off the bridge?"

"*Neh, neh!* Of course not. Ach, I'm so sorry, I should have explained." Faith panted. She felt terrible to have alarmed him, but she was winded from talking and pedaling. "When Ivy gets upset, she goes to the pond and hides under the bridge. No one knows why. Usually, she crouches on the embankment underneath it, where she's relatively safe. Our fear is she might slip and fall into the water. Like most Amish in Willow Creek, she can't swim."

The bike jerked forward as Hunter rapidly increased his pedaling again.

Touched by his unspoken concern, Faith promised, "It's going to be alright, Hunter."

"I shouldn't have let her out of my sight," he lamented. "There weren't any customers in the store. They were the ones I thought I had to watch. I never thought Ivy would leave."

"I know it's upsetting, but it's not your fault," Faith tried to comfort him as they rounded the final bend. "It happens so often Pearl gave her the nickname Wandering Ivy."

"Look! Under there!" Hunter whooped. "I see bright blue. It's her dress. Steer right, Faith, right!"

"I'm steering, I'm steering!" Faith declared, giddy with relief as she angled the handlebars to the right.

It didn't take long to coax Ivy from beneath the bridge. For one thing, the girl had neglected to put on her shawl before leaving, and the air was bitterly cold. For another, Faith promised they'd share a cream-filled doughnut when they returned, warning Ivy they'd have to hurry back before the sweets were sold out.

"Hunter Schwartz didn't want to eat dinner with Faith Yoder," Ivy mumbled as Faith took off her own shawl and wound it around Ivy's shoulders.

"That's okay," Faith patiently explained. "Men don't always like to eat dinner with women, especially if they aren't well acquainted with them. Maybe Hunter will join us one day for a special occasion after he gets to know us better. And when Ruth returns to the shop, she'll eat with us again. Until then, you may *kumme* to the bakery by yourself for your dinner break."

This compromise seemed to be acceptable to Ivy, who nodded and repeated the phrase, "Men don't always like to eat dinner with women."

"Here," Hunter said to Faith. He slipped off his coat and placed it over her shoulders. It was still warm from his body, and as she snuggled it tightly around her, she felt as if she'd received an affectionate embrace. *Such a silly thought!* she told herself. *It's no different from me letting Ivy use my shawl.*

Since Ivy didn't know how to ride a bicycle and it seemed unwise for Faith to leave her alone with Hunter since she'd just been so upset by him, the three of them sauntered back to town together. With Faith limping, Hunter pushing the bicycle and Ivy stopping every five yards to adjust her borrowed shawl, it took them over an hour to return. But at least Ivy was happy: there was one—and only one—cream-filled doughnut left in the display case.

"Denki," Faith mouthed to Pearl, who undoubtedly saved the doughnut, knowing Faith would have used it as leverage to bring Ivy back. They'd been down this road before.

Faith sighed as she heard the clock strike three. She'd have to stay at the bakery past supper time again if she was going to catch up with the baking, and Henrietta undoubtedly would have something to say about her tardiness. Still, Faith had missed dinner and she was so hungry that the apprehension she felt about eating in front of Hunter was all but forgotten.

When he came in from stowing her bike in the back, she asked, "Would you like a hot cup of *kaffi*? A little dessert after our long walk, perhaps?"

"That's kind of you to offer, but I've got to get back to the shop," he said. "I've been away from it too long. Who knows how many sales I already lost?"

As if that's my fault! Faith bristled inwardly, noticing he was standing in that wooden manner of his again, as if on guard against her friendliness, and the tenderness she'd felt toward him on their bike ride vanished.

"Well, don't let me keep you," she replied, lifting his coat from her shoulders. "And don't forget to take this."

I hardly need a man's coat wrapped around me anyway, she thought. *The ovens in my bakery will keep me plenty warm.*

Faith turned on her heel and disappeared into the kitchen before Hunter had the opportunity to thank her for her help. He stood by the table where Ivy was eating her doughnut, awkwardly holding his hat in front of him, unsure whether to wait until she finished or to leave without her.

"If you'd like, I'll see to it Ivy returns when she's finished," Pearl suggested.

"I'd appreciate that," Hunter said. He glanced

toward the kitchen, wondering if Faith might re-appear. When she didn't, he requested, "Would you please tell Faith I said *denki* for—"

He was going to say, *for helping me find Ivy*, but the young girl seemed to be absorbing his every word as she licked chocolate from the top of her treat. He didn't want to offend her by drawing attention to the fact she'd run away.

"Please tell her I said *denki* for the bicycle ride. I appreciated it that she knew where to—er, that she showed me the pond," he finished, and Pearl winked at him above Ivy's head.

Although initially the bicycle ride caused his back to knot up, the combination of pedaling and then slowly walking from the pond caused Hunter to feel more limber than he had since before he quit going to physical therapy. However, while his bodily aches lessened, his mental unease intensified. What should he tell Ivy's grandfather when he arrived to pick her up? How would he explain to Ruth sales were already down because he'd temporarily lost her employee and had to close the shop in the middle of the day? Some help he was turning out to be. His aunt would have done better to keep the shop closed—that way, she wouldn't have to pay Ivy's salary.

But his worries about what to tell Ivy's grandfather proved needless: when the clock struck five, Ivy put on her shawl and announced, "Mervin Sutter waits for me at the hitching post behind the mercantile at five o'clock." Then she walked out the door.

He wished it would be as easy to avoid telling his aunt about Ivy's escapade, but he knew Ruth would be waiting to hear how things went. He reconciled the cash with the receipt tape, checking his figures twice, and locked the money in the back room. At a minimum, he wanted to assure Ruth he'd efficiently managed the bookkeeping.

He dimmed the lights and pushed his arm through the sleeve of his coat. He hadn't noticed earlier, but the wool absorbed the smell of whatever ingredients Faith was using—cinnamon? nutmeg?—before she'd worn it this afternoon. Pausing to savor the fragrance, he noticed her storefront was closed, but a light glowed from the hall leading to the back kitchen.

He wondered if he should pop in and thank her in person for her help that afternoon. He certainly appreciated how calm and focused she'd been. Her patient kindness, both to him and then to Ivy, hadn't escaped his attention, either. He found it hard to believe someone like Faith wasn't walking out with a suitor, as Penelope implied. Perhaps because Faith was so dedicated to her business, she didn't have time for socializing? Or was it because the men in Willow Creek weren't acceptable to her? What qualities did she prefer in a suitor?

The clock struck on the half hour, jolting Hunter from his thoughts—he didn't know how his mind wandered to the subject of courting. He decided not to disrupt Faith since he'd already taken her away from her responsibilities once today. As the person who'd be making her deliveries, he wanted her to be confident he was efficient. Instead, he trekked home, glad for the cover of darkness. His spine had begun to tighten again and he walked so crookedly he feared if anyone saw him, they might assume he'd had too much to drink—something he never did.

"Hunter, *kumme* tell us all about your first day," his aunt beckoned from the parlor before he'd even latched the kitchen door behind him.

"I will, *Ant* Ruth, as soon as I tend to the stable," he stalled. "I came in to retrieve a pair of gloves first."

"If Ivy Sutter can walk from Main Street to Wheeler's Bridge without a shawl, I hardly think you need a pair of gloves to pitch hay," his aunt joshed.

Hunter poked his head into the room where his aunt and mother were giggling behind their hands like two schoolgirls.

"You heard?" he asked, his ears aflame.

"We *saw*," his mother replied, pointing to the large window, which in daylight afforded a view of the bridge and pond.

"I'm sorry, *Ant* Ruth," Hunter began. "I can explain—"

"No need to explain," his aunt protested. "I'm used to Ivy's ways and I can guess what happened."

Hunter hung his head. "But you trusted me to supervise Ivy and I failed. I wouldn't blame you if you didn't want me to—"

"You didn't fail," Ruth lectured, bending forward over her cast and pointing her finger. "You encountered a setback. That's not failure—it's life."

Hunter nodded solemnly and his aunt leaned back against the cushions again.

"The important thing is, when the challenge arose, you managed it," Ruth emphasized. "Of course, we noticed you had a little help. Faith Yoder is a very special woman. It's confounding that she's not walking out with anyone."

So, Faith wasn't being courted? Startled by the twitch of pleasure in his ribs, Hunter tempered his response. "She's a decent cyclist," he stated blandly.

"A decent cyclist?" Ruth snorted. "You and Faith sped so fast on that double bicycle, your *mamm* and I thought we'd seen a couple of wild geese flying by, didn't we, Iris?"

"*Jah*, the two of you made quite some pair!" His mother laughed exuberantly for the first time in a very long time.

In spite of his doubts he'd ever make a pair with any woman, especially not Faith Yoder, Hunter joined his aunt and mother in hearty merriment, laughing louder than both of them combined.

Chapter Four

❦

"You've gone as white as flour," Pearl commented after Faith hung up the phone on Friday shortly before noon. "Whatever is the matter?"

"That was Marianne Palmer, checking on the cupcake order for her daughter's engagement party this afternoon," Faith muttered, shaking her head in disbelief.

Pearl beamed and asked, "Did you tell her how beautiful they look? It's a *gut* thing we're allowed to take liberties with how we decorate our confections for *Englisch* customers, because I've never seen anything so fancy."

Pearl was right. The blush-pink frosting rosettes framed with white lacy ruffles was by far the daintiest, most complex design Faith had attempted for such a large order. Staying at the bakery until nine o'clock on Thursday night and arriving earlier than usual the next morning paid off: the three hundred cupcakes looked almost too pretty to eat. There was only one problem.

"I told her they're ready to be picked up," Faith answered, "but she said I promised I'd deliver them."

"You did?"

"*Neh*, of course I didn't," Faith adamantly objected.

On rare occasions, she employed one of her younger brothers to make local deliveries using their courting buggies or even the tandem bicycle if needed. But the boys worked erratic schedules during nonharvest months, both on their farm and off, and she couldn't count on them having free time in advance. She never would have committed to delivering such a large, important order to the Palmers, who lived on the other side of Willow Creek.

Pearl harrumphed. "Then she'll just have to pick them up herself."

Faith and Pearl strived to delight their customers, but Marianne had a habit of taking advantage and she could be uncompromising about her demands.

"She can't—she was calling on her way to pick up her daughter at the airport. Her husband is at home without a car, since their son is collecting the daughter's fiancé separately. The party starts at two o'clock and it's supposed to be a big surprise."

"Oh dear, I wish I could offer you my buggy, but as you know, my husband's fetching me at noon to accompany him to his doctor's appointment," Pearl apologized. "If you hurry home and retrieve your family's buggy, you should be able to make the delivery in time."

"I can't," moaned Faith. "Henrietta is using the buggy to fetch her sister from the van depot. I don't want to pedal all that way only to discover none of the other boys are home, either. I have no choice. I'll have to call a taxi."

"Ach!" Pearl's hands flew to her cheeks. "The nearest taxi will have to drive all the way from Lancaster, with the meter running. Won't that cost more than we'll earn from the cupcakes?"

"Probably, but I can't risk a dissatisfied customer, especially not such a loyal one. We fill our biggest orders for her."

"My Wayne will take you when he arrives," Pearl volunteered. "He'll be only too happy to cancel his appointment."

Faith squeezed her friend's arm, moved by her generosity. But as the business owner, this was her problem to solve, not Pearl's.

"You'll do no such thing. It's far more important for you to help your husband take care of his health than it is for me to save a few dollars.

It will all work out. But I'd better let Ivy know no one will be here for dinner today, lest she finds the bakery empty and runs away again."

"I'll call the taxi while you go tell her," Pearl proposed.

Before she reached the stoop, Faith spied Hunter through the window of the cannery. Leaning against a stool behind the cash register, he was poring over an open ledger with a serious expression on his face. It seemed he often wore a serious expression lately, quite unlike when they were younger. What was it that caused him to frown so frequently?

Yet when Faith tugged the door open, Hunter's head snapped upward and his eyes twinkled with a zest she remembered from when they were teens. It was no wonder the *meed* had been so enamored of him. At that age, girls were often taken in by any measure of attention paid to them, and Hunter's ebullient gaze made it seem as if there was no one else in the world he'd rather be speaking to.

"*Guder nammidaag*, Faith," he said, rising. "What a pleasure to have you visit the shop. How may I help you?"

In her frazzled state, Faith was so moved by his kind tone that she was momentarily at a loss for words. How many times had she asked her customers, *How may I help you?* Hearing

Hunter direct the question toward her in such a genuine manner made her forget how irritated she'd been at him the last time they parted.

"*Guder nammidaag*, Hunter. I actually came to see Ivy."

Hunter's shoulders drooped. "Mervin stopped by this morning to tell me Ivy is home sick with a cold. She won't be in tomorrow, either."

"I suppose that's what happens when she flees to the creek without a shawl," Faith said, shaking her head. Then she divulged the reason she wanted to speak to her.

"A taxi from Lancaster? That will cost a fortune!" Hunter exclaimed when he heard Faith's plan. "I took the buggy into town this morning. I'll deliver the cupcakes, but since I don't know where your customer lives, you'll have to accompany me."

"*Neh*, Hunter, that's very kind, but Pearl already called the cab company."

"Then she should call them back and cancel while I'm hitching my horse. I'll meet you in back of the bakery and we'll load the carriage there," Hunter instructed, removing the cash box from the register.

"*Neh*," Faith protested again. She was an independent woman, accustomed to addressing her business dilemmas on her own. She didn't need a man to rescue her. "I can't ask you to do that. You've got your shop to mind."

"You didn't ask—I offered. As for minding Ruth's shop, I won't close the store to take a dinner break, and I can keep it open as late as needed this evening. Besides, Ruth would want me to help. Let me stow this box and we can be on our way."

Faith opened her mouth to object a third time, but there was something so sure-minded about the look in Hunter's eyes that when he returned from the back room, she accepted his offer of assistance without further hesitation and followed him straight out the door.

As Hunter yielded off the battered side roads onto the main highway leading to the commercialized end of Willow Creek, Faith complimented his skills.

"You handle your horse expertly. If one of my brothers were making this delivery, I'd worry the cupcakes would be upside-down cakes by the time he arrived!"

Hunter didn't confide he'd perfected his technique while he was recovering from his accident, when even the smallest variation in pavement or jerking of the horse's gait could ignite his body with unspeakable pain.

Instead, he said, "*Denki*, that means a lot to

me, especially coming from someone who routinely transports *oier* on the back of a tandem bicycle."

"If you think that's impressive, you should see the tricks I can do on my unicycle," Faith quipped. They erupted with laughter and then the two of them fell into easy conversation.

Although severe back pain had kept him awake most of the previous night, causing him to take the buggy into town that morning, Hunter hardly noticed the lingering knot in his muscles as the horse carried them toward the Palmers' house. If he wasn't mistaken, Faith also appeared more carefree, giggling at his jokes and making some of her own, until eventually they pulled up at their destination: an enormous, newly constructed home situated on an elaborately manicured lawn at the end of a private lane.

"They must have a lot of *kinner*," Hunter commented nonchalantly.

"*Neh*, just two. One son and one daughter."

"That's a shame," Hunter said, thinking aloud as he brought the carriage to a halt.

"A shame? What's so shameful about that?" Faith asked in an exasperated whisper. "They're *Englisch*, not Amish. Not every family has half a dozen *kinner*."

"I only meant that they have such a large

dwelling. It seems a waste of resources when there are only four people living in it," he explained.

"Well, please keep your voice down so they don't hear you," she hissed.

Hunter didn't know what to make of Faith's sudden annoyance. He hadn't intended to distress her, nor to insult her customers. Following her to the large entryway with a tray of boxed cupcakes in his arms, he attributed the abrupt shift in her mood to nervousness: from what Faith told him, Marianne Palmer was a bit intimidating.

However, Marianne's husband, James, couldn't have been more congenial. After introducing them to two young women dressed in black-and-white uniforms, James said, "Sharon and Isabella will take the trays into the kitchen. While you're unloading the rest of the order, I'll get the checkbook. I know it's around here somewhere."

Several minutes later, James reentered the foyer just as Faith and Hunter were carrying the last of the cargo into the house.

"Here's a pad of paper, Faith," James said. "If you'll itemize a receipt, it will keep me from getting in trouble with my better half, since she's keeping track of the wedding-related expenditures. Why don't you have a seat? You look as if you could use a rest."

He pulled out an antique, elaborately carved armless walnut chair beside an equally impressive walnut desk.

"Thank you," Faith said in *Englisch*, moving toward it.

"Neh!" Hunter interjected, causing Faith to hop back. "You shouldn't sit in that chair. You might crack it."

"She might crack it?" James questioned. "That chair is made of walnut. It's a very sturdy wood."

"The wood is solid, *jah*. But look at this here," Hunter said, pointing to a barely noticeable line in the middle of the seat. "That's a hairline crack. The wood might be fine for years, or someone could sit on it at just the right angle and it would split in half."

"I never noticed that," James mused. "This chair is one of my wife's prized possessions, an heirloom from her grandmother. She'd be crushed if anything happened to it."

"I could fix it for you," Hunter offered. "My *onkel* was a master furniture restorer, and I have access to his tools and workshop. Your wife is right—it is a handsome piece. But if it's going to be used for functional purposes, it ought to be safe."

James knitted his brows. "You won't damage the original design of the chair?"

"I'd have to remove the seat in order to repair it. I'd match the epoxy to the original shade of the chair and you won't even be able to find the crack again. There'd be absolutely no damage to the design of the chair. Your wife runs a greater risk of damaging it by allowing people to sit on it in its current state. If someone puts their full weight on it—"

"Here you go, James," Faith interjected, holding out a sheet of paper. Hunter discerned by her brusque interruption she was eager to cut the discussion short so they could get back on the road, and he let the conversation drop.

After scanning the receipt, James signed a check with a flourish and tore it from his checkbook.

"Thank you, Faith. I anticipate your cupcakes will be the talk of the party," he said. Then he turned to Hunter. "I'd appreciate it if you'd fix the chair as a surprise of sorts for Marianne, and now is the perfect time to do it. My wife will be too caught up in the party to realize it's missing."

"It will be my privilege," Hunter replied.

He really meant it, too; he was itching to get his hands on a carpentry project again, even a small one. Besides, by offering to repair the chair for Faith's *Englisch* customer, he hoped to prove to her he didn't intend any disrespect to the Palmer family with his earlier remarks about their house. After agreeing on a fee, giving James his contact info and arranging a date for him to pick up the piece of furniture, Hunter hoisted the chair to his shoulder with one hand and opened the door for Faith with the other. He felt more adroit and upbeat than he had since before his accident.

Faith couldn't even look at Hunter strutting down the walk beside her like a rooster. It was disgraceful enough that he'd witnessed her splinter an entire footbridge in front of her Amish peers. But to have him point out to her *Englisch* customers that their chair wouldn't hold her weight—that was too great an indignity to bear! She took her seat in the buggy and fixed her gaze straight ahead. Hoping her cheeks didn't appear as blazing as they felt, she tried to distract herself by counting the rhythmic *clip-clop* of the horse's hooves against the pavement.

After traveling a mile in silence, Hunter said, "So, you mentioned your sister-in-law's sister is visiting for Thanksgiving?"

"Correct," Faith uttered. Her cheeks still smarted.

"That's nice. What's her name?"

"Willa. I'll introduce you if you'd like." Faith

couldn't believe Hunter was adding insult to injury by expressing interest in her sister-in-law's sister.

"Are you alright? You seem upset."

"Upset? Why would I be upset? Just because you completely embarrassed me in front of my customer, why is that any reason to be upset?" Faith blurted out.

"Embarrassed you?" Hunter looked as surprised as he sounded. "Faith, James couldn't have heard what I said about the house and even if he did—"

"It's not what you said about the house," Faith broke in, folding her arms across her chest. How could he be so dense? "It's what you said about the chair."

Hunter threw his free hand up in the air. "I honestly don't know how expressing concern about the condition of the Palmers' chair caused you any embarrassment, but I assure you, my intention was to do them—and you—a service."

He sounded so perplexed that Faith realized he truly didn't know how insulting it was that he publicly called attention to the crushing effects of her size. She had no intention of reliving the humiliation by detailing the nature of his offense.

"Never mind," she said, waving her hand. "It doesn't matter."

"It matters to me," Hunter persisted. "I wasn't being critical of their furnishings, if that's what you think, but if you believe James received my gesture as an insult, I'll apologize."

Noticing how a shadow seemed to creep over Hunter's profile, Faith suddenly questioned whether she was overreacting. After all, it wasn't Hunter's fault she was on the chubby side. And she would have been a lot more embarrassed if she'd actually broken the chair—at least he'd prevented that from happening. Faith shivered as she recognized once again Hunter was only being helpful and she'd rewarded him with a temperamental display of her own wounded pride.

What had gotten into her to act in such a way? If one of her brothers had offered to fix her customer's chair, she would have been grateful, not indignant. She had no right to lash out at Hunter as she'd done.

"*Neh*, I'm the one who needs to apologize to you, Hunter," she said in a small voice. "You showed the Palmers a kindness, just as you've shown me one by helping me make the delivery. I should have been more appreciative of your efforts. I'm sorry."

Hunter shrugged and mumbled, "It's alright."

Faith tried to think of something to ask to break the discomfiting silence that followed, but she came up blank until Hunter pulled to a stop behind the bakery.

"I'll let you off here," he indicated.

"Oh, okay," she said, although she wouldn't have minded walking back with him from the hitching post lot. "*Denki* for your help, Hunter."

"You're welcome," he duly responded and clicked for his horse to walk on.

Faith stood outside the back entry, her key poised to unlock the door, but she hesitated before going in. She felt completely deflated. The ride to the Palmers' house had been an unexpected resolution to her delivery issue, and she'd reveled in exchanging chitchat with Hunter. But on the return trip, she felt as if someone had doused them both with a bucket of ice water—and that someone was her.

She knew she couldn't fully blame her outburst on the pressures of running a business, but right then, her heart weighed like a brick within her and she wished she didn't have to enter the bakery. She wished she could run to the creek, like Ivy, or return home and help Henrietta fold laundry and mind the children. Feeling weary and alone, she prayed, *Please, Lord, give me the strength to serve my customers well. But more importantly, help me to serve You well. Forgive me for my prideful attitude and help Hunter to forgive me, too.*

It wasn't until she'd hung up her shawl and was about to wash her hands that Faith realized she was still clutching the check from James. She unfurled it and gasped at the amount. He'd given her far too much. She'd have to call and notify him of his mistake. But then she squinted to read the memo line: "cupcakes & delivery fee & well-deserved tip for both" it said in tiny print. She tapped her heels against the floorboards—she could keep it!

Well, most of it. She'd give Hunter the delivery fee, of course. She'd also give him the entire tip to demonstrate just how appreciative she really was. She wouldn't even wait to deposit the check—she removed his portion from her cash box and slipped it into an envelope, and then dashed across the street.

She burst through the door and nearly exclaimed, "Hunter, guess what!" before realizing he was helping a customer retrieve a jar from a shelf.

"Let me get that for you," he said to the diminutive Amish woman who was standing on her tiptoes beside him, her fingers wiggling to reach a large jar of corn relish. "I wouldn't want it to crash down on your head."

"Denki." She giggled, accepting his aid. "Your arms are much longer and stronger than mine."

Faith forced a cough and they both turned at once.

"Faith!" the young woman exclaimed. Her high-pitched voice was familiar, but Faith couldn't place her slender figure and delicate facial features until the woman teased, "Don't you recognize me? I'd recognize you any day. You look as healthy as ever. It's me, Willa, Henrietta's sister."

"*Jah*, of course. *Wilkom*, Willa," Faith responded haltingly. As she enfolded the young woman's tiny frame in an embrace, she couldn't help but notice how bony she'd become. "What are you doing here?"

Willa tee-heed. "I'm visiting for Thanksgiving. Didn't Henrietta tell you?"

Faith didn't know if Willa was acting kittenish for Hunter's benefit or if she really didn't understand the question. "*Neh*, I mean what are you doing in the cannery? We've put up plenty of corn relish at home."

"Really?" Willa asked innocently. "Henrietta directed me here to purchase a jar. She had items to buy at the mercantile, so we divided the errands to make them go faster. Besides, my sister knew that after being in the van for so long, I'd appreciate the opportunity to walk around and meet the *leit* of Willow Creek."

You mean the bachelors *of Willow Creek*,

Faith thought as Willa fanned her eyelashes. The arrangement smacked of Henrietta's matchmaking schemes; it was obvious Henrietta sent Willa to the cannery to meet Hunter. From Henrietta's numerous remarks, Faith knew her sister-in-law wanted Willa to find a spouse as much as she wanted Faith to find one. But there was one significant difference: Willa keenly desired to get married, whereas Faith positively did not. Especially not if it meant sharing her secret again.

Regardless, it riled Faith that Henrietta decided Willa was a more worthy candidate for Hunter's affections than Faith was, presumably because Willa was likely able to bear children. Faith was so irked to be reminded of her own physical inadequacies she couldn't drum up a single word of civility. Standing opposite the thin young woman, she sucked in her stomach and tried to remember why she'd come into the cannery in the first place.

Hunter shuffled impatiently. He'd hoped to wolf down a few bites of his dinner before the Friday afternoon tourists began streaming in, but he wouldn't have time if Faith and Willa didn't leave soon.

"If you aren't sure whether you need corn relish, I'll set it aside for you," he suggested to

Willa. "Faith can pick up the jar whenever you run low, right?"

"*Gut* idea," Faith piped up, "but before I go, may I speak with you for a moment in private, Hunter?"

He scrunched his eyebrows together. "*Jah*, alright."

When Willa looked at them askance, Faith explained, "It's about a business matter," and motioned for Hunter to follow her into the back room, where she presented him a white envelope.

"What's this?"

"It's the delivery fee for taking me to the Palmers' house," she declared, her face aglow. "Plus a tip!"

"A delivery fee? A *tip*?" Hunter repeated, deeply offended.

"*Jah*, although we don't accept tips in the bakery, sometimes the customers give us a gratuity with their large orders, which is what Mr. Palmer did today," Faith expounded, as if he didn't know what she'd meant by a tip.

Hunter stood with his mouth agape before shoving the envelope back into Faith's hand. The offer of payment for something he'd done as a...a *friend* was an affront.

"I don't want your money," he stated definitively. "And I certainly don't need a *gratuity.* I'm not your employee. Not yet, anyway."

"But Hunter, you took me all the way to the other side of Willow Creek in the middle of your working day," Faith protested. "If one of my brothers had made the delivery, I would have paid him and he would have accepted it. I don't understand—it's just a practical matter of business."

"That's what everything is to you, isn't it, Faith? Just a practical matter of business?" Hunter spouted. "Okay, then, fair is fair. I ought to have compensated *you* for taking time away from your business to find Ivy with me on Monday."

"That's entirely different and you know it," Faith countered, blinking rapidly.

Her face looked as crimson as Hunter's face felt and her shoulders sagged in apparent dejection, but it wasn't his fault her feelings were hurt. She'd brought it upon herself by being prideful, and not allowing him to help her without turning it into a financial transaction. That may have been the *Englisch* way, but it wasn't the Amish way. It wasn't the *neighborly* way.

Just then the bells on the door jangled. "Excuse me, I have customers of my own to serve now," Hunter said, grateful for the opportunity to distance himself. He stepped past Faith into the storefront, where he discovered Henrietta Yoder whispering with Willa near a display of preserves. Initially they didn't notice his presence, so he allowed them to browse while he gathered his thoughts.

Eventually, he cleared his throat. "*Guder nammidaag*, Henrietta. There was some question about whether you need relish or not. Have you made up your mind? I can ring it up for you, or if you'd prefer, I'll return it to the shelf."

"*Jah*, we'll take it, please," Henrietta replied as Faith drifted into the room. "There you are, Faith! Willa and I stopped at the bakery earlier and the store was locked. She was concerned something awful must have happened in order for you to close down your business early on a Friday."

"*Neh*," Faith answered feebly. "I had an order to deliver."

"Didn't I tell you!" Henrietta trumpeted, turning to Willa. "Didn't I say the only reason Faith would close her business in the middle of the day would be to serve another customer?"

Hunter noticed Faith's eyes flash as she responded, "That's not entirely true. We close the bakery every day for our dinner break—"

"Speaking of dinner breaks—" Henrietta snapped her fingers, as if just remembering "—I wanted to invite your *ant* and *mamm* and you to our house for Thanksgiving dinner, Hunter. I understand Ruth's abilities are limited, and rather than have your *mamm* prepare such a big meal for the three of you, we'd like you to be our guests."

Ordinarily, Hunter might have treasured celebrating Thanksgiving with the Yoder family, but after today's thorny interaction with Faith, he couldn't imagine feeling comfortable spending the better part of a day at their house.

"Denki," he replied noncommittally as he placed the relish in Henrietta's canvas bag. "I'll extend your invitation to my *ant* and *mamm*."

"Perfect!" Henrietta remarked. "We'll check back to confirm you're coming."

"I know some special games we can play in the evening," Willa suggested. "The more the merrier, I always say."

To Hunter's relief, Faith diverted their attention. *"Kumme*, Willa and Henrietta, let's continue making plans in the bakery over a mug of hot chocolate and a treat."

"None for me. I've lost weight, but I still have to control my appetite." Willa ran her hands down her hips. "I only have to look at a slice of pie and I gain three pounds."

"Then you'd better close your eyes while I eat mine," Hunter heard Faith retort as she ambled toward the door.

He didn't notice she'd left empty-handed. It wasn't until hours later when he was locking the cash box in the back room that he saw the white envelope sitting on the counter. Faith must have used his pen to inscribe a message across it:

Hunter, you earned this fair and square, so I hope you'll accept it. However, I'd rather take the money back than let go of a friendship I've had since childhood.—Faith.

He exhaled loudly. He had accused Faith of being too prideful to accept his help, but wasn't he being just as arrogant to decline the delivery fee? He peeked at the contents of the envelope. The money would definitely come in handy and he was grateful for it, but it didn't put a grin on his face the way Faith's repartee had done all the way to the Palmers' house. She was right: their friendship—yes, *friendship*—was more important than a quibble over money. Yet he couldn't quite bring himself to accept the payment, so he left it lying on the counter.

He locked the door and trod to the lot where he hitched his horse that afternoon. It took a moment for his eyes to make sense of the odd shape in the back of the buggy. When he comprehended it was the Palmers' chair, he wryly clucked his tongue. If it weren't for Faith's business, he wouldn't have any job at all, much less two. Hunter realized the furniture wasn't the only thing he needed to restore: his relationship with Faith could use repair, as well.

He clumped back toward the bakery to thank Faith and apologize for his cloddish behavior in rejecting the money. But when he reached the bakery door, there wasn't a single light on, not even in the back room.

She probably had to get home to help host Henrietta's sappy sister, he concluded. *I'll have to talk to Faith tomorrow.* Then he hurried home, eager to tell his aunt and mother they'd all been invited to the Yoders' house for Thanksgiving dinner.

Chapter Five

After setting up a narrow cot for Willa in Faith's half of the room, the young women whispered so as not to wake their small nephews on the other side of the divider.

"I know it's forward of me to ask," Willa said as she sprawled lengthwise on her bed, "but are you and Hunter walking out?"

"Of course not," Faith replied. "What would cause you to ask such a question?"

"There was a hint of tension between the two of you at the cannery this afternoon," Willa commented. "To be honest, you both wore the kind of wounded expressions people who are secretly courting wear when they've quarreled."

Although inwardly impressed by how astute Willa was to have observed the friction between Hunter and her, Faith felt no need to elaborate on the nature of their discussion.

"I assure you, we're definitely not courting," she said as she reclined and tugged the quilt to her chin. "Hunter and I are... We're business associates."

Earlier in the day, she would have referred to Hunter as a friend, but when he didn't respond to her note that afternoon, she began to question whether he held her in the same regard. She cringed to recall how expectantly she'd waited for him to visit her at the bakery, where she envisioned their making amends over a piece of dessert, or how her insides joggled each time a customer approached her doorstep.

When Hunter didn't arrive during business hours, Faith convinced herself it was because he couldn't come until the cannery was closed. She dared to hope that after locking up the shop, he might offer her a ride home, and they'd talk then. As the clock struck five, she busied herself with fastidiously wiping down tables and restocking the napkin dispensers in the storefront, so as not to appear as if she was purposely loitering until he arrived. When she finally peeked up from her chores, she noticed the cannery was dark. Hunter must have slipped out of his store without her noticing. Crestfallen, she couldn't get out the door and onto her bicycle fast enough.

"I know at least three couples in Indiana who worked together before they started courting,"

Willa prattled in a hushed tone. "Working with each other can be a *gut* way to gauge compatibility."

Although she agreed with Willa's general theory, Faith dismissed it in regard to Hunter and herself. "Be that as it may, I won't spend much time working with Hunter. He's only in town temporarily."

"You never know what might develop to make him stay," Willa insinuated. "Consider me, for example. I've just *kumme* for a visit, too, but if I found a purpose for lingering, such as the prospect of getting married and starting a family, I would."

Faith allowed Willa's reference to hang in the air without responding to it, although her mind was reeling. Willa might stay in Willow Creek? Was Henrietta designing to match Willa with Hunter as an incentive to extend her visit? Faith's thoughts took on a momentum of their own, and she tossed and turned while Willa drifted into a sound slumber.

Faith desperately wanted to turn her flashlight back on and read until she was drowsy, but she feared she'd rouse her guest or one of the children. She comforted herself with the knowledge that it wouldn't be long until she could read all night whenever she desired, provided she earned enough for the down payment on the apartment and bakery lease.

She mentally tried to calculate her earnings for the week, minus expenses and Pearl's salary, but she needed a pencil and paper to capture all the figures. Eventually, she gave up and her thoughts looped around to Willa's observation about the discord between Faith and Hunter. Faith was beginning to wonder if she'd further offended him with her note. Did he think she was overbearing? Perhaps he needed a little time to move beyond their squabble? She hoped so; otherwise, Thanksgiving dinner would feel like a long, awkward occasion instead of the worshipful and celebratory feast it was meant to be.

Slowly exhaling, she rested her hands on her stomach. She wondered how Willa lost so much weight since she'd seen her last. A prick of envy stabbed Faith's heart, and out of nowhere, she imagined Willa and Hunter walking out together. As absurd as the inkling was, she pictured their getting married, having six or eight children and building a house that wasn't "a waste of resources." Wasn't that what all men wanted, a large brood of children and a skinny wife who walked around with a baby on each hip, saying, "the more the merrier"? The very thought caused tears to stream down Faith's cheeks and into her ears. She rolled onto her side so Willa wouldn't hear her sniffing.

After a few minutes, she blotted her eyes with the end of her pillowcase. She was being ridiculous, contriving these outlandish scenarios. Besides, whoever Hunter and Willa walked out with or married was none of Faith's concern. Unlike Willa, Faith didn't need a husband—especially not one as bullheaded as Hunter—to make her feel as if she had purpose in Willow Creek. Faith had customers to serve and a financial deadline to meet, and what she really needed was a good night's rest so her emotions wouldn't get the best of her again.

Indeed, the next morning as she careened into town on her bike, she felt entirely refreshed. Saturday was always a bustling day in the bakery, and the Saturday before Thanksgiving promised to be their busiest day yet. She was always energized by her customers' appreciation and good cheer, particularly around the holidays, when she enjoyed meeting people whose travels took them through Willow Creek.

Between working the counter, answering the phone and baking new treats, Faith and Pearl barely had a moment to speak to each other until it was time for dinner.

"Since Ivy will be out sick again today, perhaps we should work through our dinner break this afternoon?" Pearl suggested.

Faith replaced an empty tray of sticky buns with a full one. Although she was tempted to take Pearl up on the offer, Faith knew it would be counterproductive to skip their dinner break. Henrietta could imply what she would, but Faith wasn't so driven to make a sale that she'd deny Pearl and herself a much-needed rest.

"*Neh*, we deserve to put our feet up for a bit. Besides, I want to hear how your husband's appointment went yesterday."

They changed the sign on the door to Closed, lowered the lights and retrieved their lunchboxes from the back room before bowing their heads to say grace. As they ate, Faith apprised Pearl of the outcome of the Palmer delivery, and Pearl reported the doctor said her husband's blood pressure reading was out of the danger zone.

"Praise *Gott*!" Faith's voice reverberated in the empty room.

"I only wish Ruth Graber's health was improving, too," Pearl remarked.

Faith wrinkled her forehead. "I thought her recovery was progressing nicely."

"Well, we stopped at her place last evening and she said the doctor had paid her a house call. He was concerned about the results of blood tests he'd done when she went to the emergency room. So, although her bones are healing nicely, she's been advised to get more rest. From what I gather, she isn't supposed to go out and about in the buggy, either. Something about her lungs and the cold weather…"

"What a shame. If I know Ruth, she must feel cooped in. Just yesterday Henrietta invited her to our house for Thanksgiving. I guess that means she won't be able to *kumme*."

"Ach! Where's my head? They mentioned that to me last night. I was supposed to convey the message Hunter will be the only one attending. Iris doesn't want to leave Ruth alone, but she insisted Hunter should go by himself."

Faith was nonplussed. Did Hunter truly wish to spend Thanksgiving with the Yoder family, or had he been put on the spot and felt obligated to accept the invitation?

"Ruth and Iris are going to spend Thanksgiving alone?" Having dined with Ruth nearly every day for the past two years, Faith was aware of how much pleasure the older woman derived from eating together. She supposed Ruth had to eat alone so often at home that she prized the chance to gather around the table with others. It was a shame she'd miss celebrating Thanksgiving at the Yoder farm.

"It doesn't seem fair, does it? Since my *kinner* aren't coming to visit until *Grischtdaag*, and Wayne and I will be alone, too, I considered offering to go to Ruth's, but I couldn't invite myself, could I?"

"*Neh*… But what if you and I were to cook dinner here at the bakery and bring it to Ruth and Iris? That wouldn't be the same as inviting ourselves to be their guests. Perhaps we could ask Ivy and her *groossdaadi* to join us, too?"

"Ruth would love that!" Pearl joyfully waved her spoon. "But only if it's okay with Henrietta that you won't be home to help with your family's dinner preparations."

"Willa will be there to take my place—she can give Henrietta and Lovina a hand with whatever needs to be done," Faith reasoned earnestly. "Besides, both Ruth and Iris's husbands are deceased, and *Gott's* Word instructs us to honor widows. Henrietta can't argue with that."

And this way, Faith rationalized to herself, *Willa can have Hunter all to herself, which is whom I assume she really meant when she said, "the more the merrier."* As for Hunter, Faith reckoned he'd barely notice her absence anyway.

Hunter racked his brain for a way to show Faith he was sorry for his lack of humility the day before, but even apologizing for being prideful sounded, well, prideful. He finally decided he'd pay her a visit at the bakery and let her know he was looking forward to spending Thanksgiving with her and her family. Perhaps he'd order a few of the apple fry pies he'd heard so much about and bring them home to his aunt and mother. But every time he attempted to lock the cannery, another customer entered. He didn't want to turn away business, so he resigned himself to waiting until after closing time.

When the hour came, he noted the crowd of customers still milling about in Faith's storefront, so he meandered to the mercantile, where he was inspired to purchase a packet of batteries for her bicycle headlamp. Exultant at having found the perfect token to give Faith when he expressed his regret, Hunter charged out the door, nearly barreling into Joseph Schrock, his wife, Amity, and Amity's visiting parents. Hunter refrained from tapping his foot as introductions were made and details about holiday plans were exchanged. Finally, the group bid him a joyous Thanksgiving, but it was too late: Faith's bakery was empty and its lights were off. Hunter slid the batteries beneath the breast of his jacket and trudged home.

After serving customers by himself all day, he had a new appreciation for Ivy's assiduousness. His muscles burned, and he was relieved the next day was an "off Sunday," meaning the *leit* didn't congregate for church. Rather, they held private worship services in their own homes. After Sunday dinner, he was so exhausted he excused himself for a brief nap but ended up sleeping right through another visit from Pearl and Wayne.

"Isn't that kind?" his aunt was remarking to his mother in the parlor when he got up.

"Indeed," his mother replied. To Hunter, she explained, "Pearl and Faith offered to prepare Thanksgiving dinner for your *ant* and me. They planned to make it at the bakery and deliver it to us, but we thought it would be better to cook it here, where I can help. Faith will make the pies in her bakery in the morning, so as to be out of Henrietta's way. Ivy and Mervin Sutter are also invited."

"Faith won't be eating at her own home?" Hunter asked.

"Uh-oh, do I detect a note of disappointment?" Ruth teased. "We thought you'd enjoy dining with your young male friends for a change, but if it's Faith's company you're interested in keeping, tell Henrietta you've changed your mind and you'll be staying here with us."

"*Neh*, it's…it's not that—" Hunter stammered. "I'm surprised she wouldn't want to be with her family, that's all."

Yet he couldn't deny a sense of disappointment that Faith wouldn't be present at her family's celebration. He also couldn't help but wonder if she was deliberately avoiding him. Not that he would have blamed her—she probably wondered why he still hadn't acknowledged her note.

He decided he'd visit her at the first opportunity, but Monday and Tuesday were so busy at the cannery, he didn't have a moment to pull himself away from the shop. Before he knew it, it was four fifty-five on Wednesday afternoon.

"On Thursday I'm eating Thanksgiving dinner at Ruth Graber's house," Ivy announced, just as she'd announced on Monday and Tuesday afternoons.

"That's right, Ivy." Hunter smiled.

"Faith Yoder is making dessert," Ivy informed him.

"Her pies are bound to be *appenditlich*. I hope I have treats that taste as *gut* as at Henrietta's house."

"*Neh*, you're eating at Ruth Graber's house with Faith Yoder."

Hunter cocked his head to the side. He didn't want to upset Ivy by contradicting her, but she was so particular about details that he wondered why she thought he was eating at Ruth's.

"You mean after dinner, I'll come back to Ruth's house for leftover dessert, right?" he asked.

"*Neh*, you're eating Thanksgiving dinner at Ruth Graber's house. One thirty on Thursday."

Hunter pressed her for clarification. "Ivy, who told you that?"

"Willa Gingerich from Indiana."

The conversation was confusing, even for him, but he shouldn't have been surprised Ivy kept everyone's names straight. She seldom erred with memorizing names or numbers.

"Well, that's almost right, but not quite," Hunter explained. "Willa Gingerich from Indiana invited me to eat at Henrietta Yoder's house."

"*Jah*. Willa Gingerich from Indiana invited Hunter Schwartz to eat dinner at Henrietta Yoder's house," Ivy repeated, and Hunter breathed a sigh of relief. She had the story straight.

Then she added, "I told Willa Gingerich *neh*. Hunter Schwartz is eating dinner at Ruth Graber's house with Faith Yoder. One thirty on Thursday. Thanksgiving Day, a special occasion."

Recalling how Faith told Ivy that he might eat with them on a special occasion, Hunter's mouth fell open. "When, Ivy? When did you tell this to Willa?"

"Three thirty. Willa Gingerich purchased one jar of sweet mustard. Four dollars. Exact change."

Three thirty *today*? Hunter must have stepped out to use the washroom at the very moment Willa stopped in for the mustard. Henrietta's sister was probably nattering on to Ivy about Thanksgiving dinner and that's when the misunderstanding arose. Hunter was so flabbergasted he couldn't speak.

"Mervin Sutter waits for me at the hitching post behind the mercantile at five o'clock," Ivy stated as the clock tolled, leaving Hunter alone to shake his head in silence.

Now what was he going to do? If he sprinted to the bakery to explain the situation to Faith and tell her he was still planning to go to the farm, it would look as if he was going out of his way not to keep company with her on Thanksgiving. But if he let the misunderstanding rest, the Yoder family might assume he changed his plans just to be with Faith.

Hunter had met *meed* like Willa who would conclude he was interested in Faith romantically. Not that courting Faith wouldn't have appealed to him under different circumstances, but Hunter knew he was in no condition, physically or financially, to be anyone's suitor. No, he had to explain; he just hoped with the recent friction between Faith and him, she'd see the humorous side of the situation.

But the laugh appeared to be on Hunter, because by the time he locked his shop and started across the street, the bakery was already deserted. Adjusting his hat to protect his ears from the cold, Hunter supposed there were far worse things than spending Thanksgiving at Ruth's house with Faith. He only hoped Faith felt the same way about spending the holiday with him.

Faith figured by closing her shop half an hour early on Wednesday and returning home to make the pies and rolls for her family's Thanksgiving dinner, she'd demonstrate she really did value the time she spent with Henrietta and Willa. But after everyone finished eating supper and the women were left alone to clear and clean the dishes, Faith could hardly get a word out of the two sisters.

Finally, she commented, "It's so quiet I can hear the clock ticking in the parlor. Are you upset with me because I'm not going to be home for Thanksgiving dinner?"

"*Neh*, not at all," Henrietta claimed. "We'll miss having you here, but I think it's *wunderbaar* you're showing hospitality to Ruth and Pearl, and Ivy and her *groossdaadi*."

"You forgot to mention Hunter and his

mamm." Willa sulked, circling the bottom of a bowl with a dish towel.

"*Jah*, I'll be celebrating the holiday with Hunter's *mamm*, but not with Hunter—he'll be eating with you," Faith corrected her.

Henrietta winked at Faith. "It's alright, you don't have to pretend you're not courting. Ivy told Willa today Hunter wants to have dinner with you instead of coming here. Don't worry, your secret is safe with us."

Faith suspended a dirty pot above the dishwater, too stunned to move. She didn't know for certain what Ivy told Willa, but she didn't have to know: based on her knowledge of Ivy's communication skills, Faith could guess the gist of what transpired.

"I'm afraid Ivy was speaking out of turn," she explained. "She didn't know what she was talking about."

"*Neh*, Ivy was very clear about what she was saying." Willa pouted. "I only wish you'd been more honest about your interest in Hunter before I got my hopes up."

"Willa!" Henrietta intervened with a sternness that surprised Faith. "You know how discreet most Amish couples are about their courtships. Faith has done nothing wrong by keeping her relationship private. Besides, you can have your pick of suitors at home—Hunter may be Faith's only option here in Willow Creek. Now if you'll excuse me, I need to put the boys to bed, fold the laundry and then finish the cleaning I didn't get to do this afternoon."

Abashed, Faith plunged the pot into the soapy water. The nerve of her sister-in-law to insist Faith and Hunter were courting, when Faith specifically denied it! And didn't Henrietta understand how hurtful it was to hear her announce Faith's courtship options were limited, whereas Willa's were limitless? Ironically, Faith knew if she pointed out her sister-in-law's insensitivity, Henrietta's own feelings would be hurt, since she truly believed she was standing up for Faith. Instead of responding aloud, Faith nearly scoured a hole right through the copper-bottomed pot.

Eventually, to Faith's chagrin, Willa acquiesced. "I suppose Henrietta has a point. I'm sorry, Faith—I was being selfish. Now, would you like my help making the pies?"

"Definitely not!" Faith barked. Then, recognizing how cross she sounded, she forced a joke. "You said you gain weight just looking at pies, so I wouldn't want to tempt you. I think that's what happens to me—one minute I'm measuring ingredients, the next minute, I've eaten a third of a pie!"

"You're blessed to have found a suitor who doesn't mind that you're carrying a few extra pounds."

Faith held her tongue as she retrieved a bowl of eggs from the icebox. *Please*, Gott, *help me turn the other cheek*, she silently prayed.

"I *haven't* found a suitor," she iterated. "But you've done very well to lose so much weight, Willa. Are you following a special meal plan?"

"Neh." The normally talkative Willa went silent as she tugged a cupboard door open, shielding her face. After stacking the dry plates inside, she closed the door and confided, "I just lost my appetite for a while about a year ago."

Faith could tell by the way Willa wouldn't meet her eyes that she was embarrassed by whatever triggered her weight loss. "I didn't mean to pry," she said. "You don't have to talk about it."

"It's alright," Willa responded, draping the damp dishcloth over the rack to dry. Lowering her voice, she confided, "You see, I started losing weight because my suitor said I was getting too fat."

"Really?" Faith was appalled. "He actually told you that?"

"Not in so many words, *neh*, but one time

he was embracing me and he whispered, 'my plump, darling heifer,' into my ear and then he sort of laughed."

"Willa! He didn't!" Faith yelped, and then quickly cupped her hand over her mouth. In a quieter tone, she admitted, "I would have been livid!"

Willa shrugged. "I was more hurt than angry, especially since I hadn't ever allowed him to hug me before then because I was self-conscious about my size. He said he meant it as a term of endearment and that I was being overly sensitive. It was true, I *was* overweight, so I tried not to let it bother me when he kept calling me that, but I felt so… I don't know, *unwomanly* somehow. I completely lost my appetite. If you can believe it, I became so depressed, I had to force myself to eat!" Her face was beet red as she half laughed, half choked at the memory.

Faith understood how devastating it was to be vulnerable with a suitor, only to have him respond in a crushing manner. "I'm so sorry his comment affected you like that, Willa."

"Does Hunter make critical remarks about your weight?"

Faith blew air through her lips. Was there any sense trying to convince Willa that Hunter wasn't courting her? Faith decided just to answer Willa's question.

"*Neh*, Hunter never says anything critical about my weight," she replied, suddenly realizing he never directly *said* anything about her weight at all. Was it possible the awkward feelings she had about her size in Hunter's presence actually originated in Faith's own mind and she wrongly attributed them to him? Could it be she jumped to other conclusions about him that were inaccurate, too? Perhaps she'd been too quick to assume his lack of communication lately meant he didn't care about their friendship—was it possible he'd just been too busy to respond to her note?

"I don't think I'd continue to walk out with a suitor who put me down," Faith continued, "even if his comments were supposedly truthful or affectionate or made in jest."

"Neither would I," Willa said, smugness curling her mouth. "But it took me a while to get to that point. Once my confidence returned, I told him I'd rather walk barefoot through a field of cow pies than walk out with him any longer because he had no idea how to treat a lady!"

The two young women clutched each other's arms as they giggled. When they straightened, Faith wiped her eyes with the corner of her apron and suggested she'd be pleased if Willa would roll the pie crusts while Faith measured the fillings. Their four hands made light work of the process, and when Henrietta rejoined them hours later, they were sliding the final pies into the oven.

"Mmm," Willa said, closing her eyes and breathing in. "The aroma is my favorite part of baking."

"Leftovers are my favorite part of baking," Henrietta remarked. "There's enough here so I won't have to bake again for days."

"*Eating* is my favorite part of baking," Faith admitted, accidentally dropping an empty pie tin, which clattered raucously against the floor.

When the men rushed into the kitchen to see what the commotion was about, they found the three women doubled over in laughter.

"Are you alright?" Mason asked.

"We're fine," Faith said. "*Kumme*, everyone grab a fork. It's neither too late for pie nor too early to give thanks."

The way Faith saw it, she was doubly blessed, and she wasn't going to wait until Thanksgiving to express her gratitude to God. As she sliced into the warm golden crust, she silently prayed. *Lord*, denki *for this time with my family tonight and for the fellowship I'll have with my friends at Ruth's house tomorrow.*

That evening, when Hunter told his aunt and mother what Ivy communicated to Willa, Ruth raised an eyebrow at Iris.

"Our Ivy is more insightful than folks give her credit for," Ruth said.

"What's that supposed to mean?" Hunter heard the defensiveness in his own voice.

"It means we'll be glad to set a place for you at the table tomorrow," his mother responded, giving her son's arm a squeeze.

"This works out better anyway," Ruth declared. "I was going to ask Wayne to pick up Faith and her pies from the bakery in time for our devotions before dinner, but this way, Hunter can get her."

Hunter knew it was useless to resist Ruth's overt matchmaking attempts, and besides, he welcomed the opportunity to clear the air with Faith in private. He'd already set off for town the next day when he realized he'd forgotten the batteries he purchased for her, but he didn't want to draw attention to his gift by returning home, so he rode on. Since Main Street was virtually deserted, Hunter pulled up in front of the bakery and rapped on the glass pane of the door.

Faith quickly appeared, gliding into the square of sunshine to unlock the door. She was wearing a verdant green dress that accentuated the green flecks in her hazel eyes, and her hair glinted in the light.

"Happy Thanksgiving, Hunter," she greeted

him, grinning mischievously. "I assume you're here to court me?"

Hunter faltered backward and nearly tumbled down the stairs.

"Ach! Be careful." Faith giggled as he regained his balance. "I was kidding! I heard what Ivy told Willa, and if your *ant* and *mamm* are anything like my sister-in-law, we've both been hearing the same farfetched insinuations about our relationship. I thought by making light of it, I'd put your mind at ease. Don't worry, I know we consider ourselves to be business associates."

"Business associates, that we are," Hunter confirmed. He cleared his throat and added, "But we're friends, too, right?"

Faith's eyes twinkled as she gave him a single, decisive nod. "Since childhood."

Hunter's shoulders relaxed. "Actually, I was trying to think of a way I could put *your* mind at ease," he confessed. "Not just about Ivy's mix-up, but about my behavior the other day. I tried several times to apologize, but I kept missing you. I'm sorry for not accepting the delivery fee. Sometimes I can be as stubborn as a mule."

Faith tittered. "That makes two of us. Now, speaking of deliveries, could you please give me a hand with the trays in the back room?"

They secured the dinner rolls and pies in the

back of the buggy and took their seats in front. Because their tradition was to fast on Thanksgiving morning, the smell made Hunter's mouth water. "I'm tempted to dig into those pies this very instant," he said. "What kind are you holding on your lap?"

"I hate to disappoint you, but it's not a pie. It's a pumpkin roll," Faith teased.

"With pecans on top?"

"Of course."

"Mmm," he moaned, licking his lips. "That's how Justine always made them."

"Who's Justine?"

Hunter was so hungry he hadn't realized he'd spoken aloud. "Er, she was someone I courted, but it was a while ago," he answered vaguely before redirecting the conversation. "How many pumpkin rolls did you sell before the holiday?"

"I'm not sure I remember off the top of my head," Faith said with a sigh. "In fact, I'm not sure I've even logged the amount. Paperwork is not my specialty, I'm afraid."

"As long as you're turning a profit, I suppose that's what matters."

"*Jah*, I suppose," Faith replied.

"But?" Hunter pushed, sensing she had more to say.

"But I'm not sure I *am* turning a profit. To be honest, my books are riddled with errors. I keep trying to balance the figures, but I must be doing something wrong. I wouldn't be so worried if I didn't have to put a down payment on the lease by the first of the year, for both the bakery and the apartment upstairs. I'm not sure I'm going to make it, but I hardly have a moment to stop and assess the numbers."

As Faith spoke, her voice began to tremble, and Hunter briefly felt an impulse to wrap his arm around her shoulder.

"Trust me," he said in a quiet voice, "I understand what a burden it can be to carry a financial pressure alone."

Faith turned toward him, sheepishly rolling her eyes. "Listen to me, complaining about finances on a holiday! I'm sorry, Hunter. My sister-in-law is right—my priorities aren't where they should be. She says I am too focused on my business."

"You needn't apologize," Hunter argued. "If you'll allow me, I'll look over your books for you. But there is one condition."

Faith's face brightened. "Of course, what is it?"

Hunter delivered his condition carefully but firmly, "You mustn't offer me payment. This is something I want to do for you as…as your friend."

"But if it interrupts your working day—"

"It won't. Tomorrow morning is my first

round of deliveries. I'll arrive early to review your accounting. How does five thirty sound?"

"That would be *wunderbaar*, Hunter," Faith acknowledged. "But the very least I can do is make you breakfast."

"Agreed." Hunter nodded. "Would you like me to bring my own *oier*, or can you transport some yourself?"

"I'll transport them myself," she said with a nudge to his arm. "But if I should wobble into a ditch, we'll have to eat them scrambled."

Even as he was laughing, it occurred to Hunter that Ruth was right: Ivy was more insightful than people gave her credit for. That day, he was so thankful to be among his family and friends, he hardly noticed the pain in his lower back, hip and legs. And when he bit into the pumpkin roll Faith served, every memory of Justine and the past vanished. All he could taste was the goodness of the here and now on his lips.

Chapter Six

As Faith unlocked the back door to the bakery at four thirty on Friday morning, she felt her stomach rumble. After Thanksgiving dinner and dessert at Ruth's, followed by a round of leftovers when Hunter brought her back to her own house and stayed for supper, and then more dessert while they played games with her family, Faith didn't think she'd be hungry again for days.

She decided it must be the morning air stirring her appetite. Shivering, she turned up the heat in the bakery. As unseasonably cold as the temperature was, she was grateful it hadn't snowed yet, which would mean she'd have to walk instead of ride her bike to the bakery. She hoped the inclement weather would hold off until after Christmas, when she'd be settled into her apartment and wouldn't have to worry about trekking into town in frigid conditions.

Once the room warmed, she began preparing the bread dough to rise before turning her attention to the display shelf. In her haste to get home early on Wednesday evening, she neglected to wrap several trays of goodies. They'd gone dry and most of them would have to be moved to the day-old shelf. She also marked down the price of two pies that hadn't sold. How was she going to make a profit if she was so careless with her products? She sighed and focused on mixing the ingredients for molasses gingerbread cookies, which she'd come in especially early to make to send with Hunter to the Piney Hill festival.

She was concentrating so hard on what she was doing, an hour later she didn't notice Hunter standing inside the back entrance until he cleared his throat.

"*Guder mariye*, Faith," he spoke softly, sweeping his hat from his head. Her eyes traveled from his thick, curly hair, down the masculine lines of his cheekbones, and lingered on the distinctive cleft in his chin.

"*Guder mariye*," she replied, embarrassed she'd been staring. "You startled me."

"The door was unlocked, so when you didn't hear me knocking, I came in," he explained, his brows crimped together. "If you don't mind my saying so, you really should bolt the door when you're here alone."

"As you'll soon discover from my ledger, there's not much to steal," Faith joshed, "unless someone wants day-old bread, in which case, they're welcome to it."

"It's not your money I'm worried about," Hunter responded, the frown lines in his forehead deepening. "A woman working alone in the early morning hours—"

Faith flattened a lump of cookie dough with the rolling pin. While she was touched by Hunter's concern, his advice was unnecessary. She was strong. She knew how to take care of herself. She'd better; after all, she was going to be doing it for the rest of her life.

"*Denki* for your concern, but I doubt anyone in their right mind would trouble a sturdy Amish woman wielding one of these!" she said as she waved the rolling pin. She was half kidding. The Amish practiced nonviolence and she couldn't imagine ever physically striking another person, but that was her point: she doubted she'd ever need to. "Besides, I usually do lock the door, but I must have forgotten. Please, take off your coat. Would you like breakfast now or after you've finished reviewing my finances?"

"After I've finished. I'm not hungry yet. I confess, when I returned from your house last evening, I devoured another slice of pumpkin roll."

"Really? That must have been your third piece!"

"My fourth," he confessed. "What can I say? I know a *gut* thing when I have it."

Faith felt her cheeks go rosy. "I'm glad you enjoyed it. Now, I'll put on a pot of *kaffi*. Would you like to work at that little desk over in the corner, or would you prefer to work at a table in the storefront?"

"I'll work at this desk," he replied. "If you turn the lights on in the storefront, someone might think the bakery is open."

Although she hardly spoke to Hunter except to answer questions he had about her calculations, Faith enjoyed his presence nearby as she baked. There was something cozy about being in the same room with him while working on separate tasks that felt different from when she baked with Pearl. About an hour before the bakery was scheduled to open, she heard a persistent knocking on the front door.

"Early bird customers," she explained to Hunter. "Usually, we'd make them wait, but as you can probably tell from my books, I need all the business I can get. I'll be right back."

Through the glass pane she saw three young *Englisch* men wearing jackets with a nearby college's insignia on them, huddled on the front step. Two of them appeared to be holding up the third, and Faith raced to the door, concerned he was injured.

She was so flustered that she spoke in *Deitsch* instead of *Englisch*. "Is he hurt?"

The young man who was being propped up raised his head and jeered in a slurred voice, "I must be worse off than I thought because I didn't understand a word she just said."

He and the boy on his right both howled, but the man on his left apologized, "I'm very sorry, miss, but could we purchase a cup of coffee and some bagels? He really needs to get some food into his system."

Faith hesitated. The young man reeked of alcohol. Had he been drinking all night or had he just begun? She was aware of how dangerous the effects of alcohol consumption could be.

"*Jah*," she said, allowing them entrance to the bakery, "but I don't sell bagels, so you'll have to make another selection. How do you take your *kaffi*?"

"*Kaffi*," snorted the drunk man. "Did you hear the way she said *coffee*?" He staggered as his friends eased him into a chair, before adding, "I take it piping hot and extra sweet, just like you."

Although her hands were trembling, Faith

spooned sugar into the cup and secured the lid. In the most authoritative voice she could muster, she stated to the other two men, "You may have this complimentary cup of *kaffi*, along with a few honey bars to counter the effects of the alcohol, but I don't want you to stay in the bakery. Please take your friend and leave."

"You can't kick us out!" the drunk man bellowed. "I'll complain to your manager. What's his name?"

"My name is Faith and *I'm* the manager. This is my bakery and I want you to leave," Faith repeated, placing her hands on her hips and glaring at him. "Now, please."

The drunken man slapped his thigh. "Look—her face is turning as red as her hair!"

Faith's throat burned. She was torn between wanting the floor to swallow her up and wanting to give the man a verbal chewing out he wouldn't soon forget.

Hunter stepped into the storefront and said in a deep, commanding voice, "Faith asked you to leave, so you need to get going. This instant."

"Who's going to make me, farm boy?" the young man ridiculed. He wobbled upon rising from the chair.

Hunter had wrangled calves that were more robust than this college kid and he advanced forward, but his Amish beliefs prohibited him from physically assisting the boy out the door.

"Shut up, Bill," the smaller of the two other men ordered, grabbing his friend's arm and steering him toward the door, nervously eyeing Hunter over his shoulder. "We're going."

The third student stepped forward to take the cardboard tray of coffee and goodies Faith had prepared. "I'm very sorry, miss, sir," he said and scampered toward the exit.

Crossing the room to relock the door behind the unwelcome patrons, Hunter noticed the last one to leave placed a crumpled wad of bills on the far tabletop. He picked it up.

"I assume this is supposed to make up for their coarse behavior," he said incredulously.

But when he turned around, he realized Faith had retreated into the kitchen. He spotted her at the sink, washing her hands.

"Why did you do that?" she asked. Her head was angled so he couldn't read her expression, but her tone was one of resentment.

Hunter was dumbfounded. "Do what?"

"You're here to reconcile my accounting, not to interfere with my interactions with my customers."

"Are you joking?" Hunter brayed. "Faith, that man was drunk. He was harassing you.

You don't know what might have happened if I hadn't told them to leave."

Faith vigorously scrubbed her fingernails with a brush beneath a torrent of water that was so hot steam was rising from her skin.

"I know how big your muscles are, Hunter, and how much you pride yourself on your physical strength, but *Gott* would have protected me. Besides, I'm a strong woman. I can look after myself."

Pride in his physical strength? Faith had no idea just how weak Hunter felt! That very morning it had taken him five minutes to put on his trousers because his hips and legs were so tight he could hardly lift his feet from the floor.

But since he wasn't about to confide that in her, he spat out the words, "You're not as strong as you think you are, Faith. You're just f—"

He was about to tell her she was just foolish, but remembering what *Gott's* Word said about calling anyone a fool, he held his tongue.

"I'm just *what*, Hunter?" Faith challenged. Now she was scrubbing the skin in between her fingers. "I'm not strong, I'm just *fat*, right? Go ahead—you're not the first to think it and you won't be the last!"

"What? *Neh*," Hunter protested. He didn't know why on earth Faith would imagine that was what he was thinking. "I was going to say you're just *foolhardy*. You may believe you're strong enough to overcome someone who wishes to do you harm, but you don't know what some men can be like. When they're around a becoming woman like you, they exhibit barnyard behavior—"

Faith's sobs interrupted what he was going to say. Her torso shook with the intensity of them, but she didn't stop cleansing her hands and she kept her face averted. As Hunter watched her quaking profile, he realized she wasn't really mad at him. She was upset by what had just transpired and she was trying to wash the incident away.

He gingerly walked to her side and turned off the water. Picking up a dish towel, he reached for her hand. She allowed him to lift her arm, but she wouldn't look him in the eye. Very carefully, he patted her palms and fingers dry and gently placed her hand by her side. Then he reached for her other hand and dried that one, too. Finally, she lifted her chin upward and sighed. He handed her the cloth so she could wipe the tears from her cheeks and dab the skin beneath her eyes.

She blinked her long, reddish lashes twice before directly meeting his gaze. "*Denki*, Hunter. For everything."

He knew she was thanking him for guarding her as well as comforting her, and the appreciation and admiration in her eyes reminded him of how he used to feel when Justine complimented his abilities, only better, because he never thought he'd feel that capable again. He humbly replied, "I'm glad I can help."

"I'll get started making breakfast now," she stated practically.

"I'd like that. We can discuss my findings while we're eating, and then I'll be on my way to Piney Hill."

After Faith served them each a plate heaped with breakfast scrapple, orange slices and toast made from freshly baked bread, Hunter said grace.

"*Gott*, we thank You for Your provision in this meal as well as for Your protection in our lives. Please help us to forgive those who trespass against us, just as Christ has forgiven us our trespasses."

"Amen!" Faith confirmed loudly. Then, a few bites into their meal, she asked the question he'd been dreading. "So, will I have enough money to make the down payment by the first of the year?"

Faith could tell Hunter was stalling by the deliberate way he was chewing his food. She knew the answer wasn't good, and she braced herself for his response. She had already cried in front of him once this morning. She appreciated how tender and respectful he'd been in response to her outburst, but she wouldn't allow herself to break down again.

"Well, based on your records and your projections for the rest of the season," he hesitated, "it looks as if you may fall a bit short of your goal."

"How short?"

"Twelve to eighteen hundred dollars."

"Twelve to eighteen hundred dollars!" Faith yipped. "The landlord won't renew the lease if I'm even *two* hundred dollars short! My future depends on the bakery—I can't lose it, I just can't!"

Hunter narrowed his eyes. "I know it's not the answer you wanted to hear, Faith, but I had to be honest with you about my calculations. There still may be ways to meet your goal, but if not, I'm certain *Gott* has a plan for your future, whether or not you keep the bakery."

Faith kept her eyes from overflowing by focusing on separating a triangle of orange from its rind. Hunter had no idea why it was so important for her to keep her business, and she would never tell him. But, as upset as she was, she recognized the ultimate truth in what he was saying: her future depended on God, not on the bakery itself.

"You're right," she agreed solemnly. "I believe *Gott* has a plan for my future, even though I may not know what that is yet. I only know for now, He has provided me this bakery, which I treasure. I still have several weeks to meet my financial goal, so, with *Gott's* help, I'd like to do everything I can to make the down payment."

Hunter rubbed his chin. "Alright, let's discuss ways you might do that."

As they ate their breakfast and Faith bagged up the goodies for the festival, they volleyed ideas about how she could increase her revenue. Having worked for an *Englisch* company, Hunter was more familiar with practices that appealed to *Englischers*, and he brought a fresh approach to their brainstorming session.

"Have you considered keeping the bakery open later?"

"Ordinarily, I might," Faith said. "But my concern is Henrietta doesn't think I spend enough time with my family as it is. Who knows what she'd say if I came home later than I already do?"

As soon as she spoke, Faith felt a stitch of guilt. She hadn't meant to air her sister-in-law's grievance, but it was so easy to be open with Hunter that the words just slipped out. She quickly added, "To be fair, she has a point. On occasion I wish I could spend more time at home, too. Regardless, I don't think my in-store bakery sales would be significant enough to justify extended hours. I earn the most money on large orders my regular *Englisch* customers place for holidays and other special celebrations. I wish I could increase those sales."

Hunter scratched his chin. "Well, *Grischtdaag* and New Year's Eve are coming up, and *Englischers* are known to throw big parties, both at home and at work, with lots of food," he said. "What do you do to advertise to the *Englisch* community?"

"I've requested if *Englisch* customers enjoy my goods and services they'd spread the word to their friends in neighboring towns, but I'm afraid…" Realizing it would be immodest to complete her thought, Faith allowed her sentence to trail off.

Hunter pushed her to finish it. "You're afraid what?" he asked. Faith noticed that about him: he was genuinely interested in her opinions, especially those she was most hesitant to express.

"It's puffed up of me to say, but I'm afraid some of them, like Marianne Palmer, might not want to 'share' me—those are her words, not mine. I don't know if I could actually count on them to tell others about the bakery."

"Well, I think you should keep asking customers to tell others about your shop," Hunter advised. "But meanwhile, look at that box you're holding."

Faith glanced at the plain white cardboard box. What was wrong with it? She shrugged in confusion.

"You don't have your business name, hours and phone number on it," Hunter explained. "The *Ordnung* for Willow Creek doesn't prohibit including that information on your packaging, does it?"

"*Neh*, provided it's simple, not ornamental, and it doesn't contain any graven images," Faith confirmed. "I considered having boxes and bags printed for the bakery, but I discovered it was more costly than I anticipated. I'm not sure it would be worth the investment, especially when every penny counts."

"Hmm… Labels are cheap. Could you affix labels to your boxes and bags? There's a printing shop on the other side—"

"Of Willow Creek! I know the place," Faith exclaimed. "That's a fantastic plan, Hunter."

His eyes were alight as he replied, "I'll go right past the printer when I make the delivery to Piney Hill. If you jot down your information, I can take it to the printer this morning."

"Really? You'd do that for me?" Faith meant to express her gratitude, but she realized her choice of words might make Hunter think she was playing coy, so she quickly elaborated, "I mean, I'd really appreciate it."

Hunter grinned. "We're business partners, aren't we? Your success is my success and mine is yours. Speaking of which, I'd better get on the road to the festival."

Faith was so absorbed in their conversation she hadn't realized how late it was getting. "Of course. I'll finish packaging these while you bring your buggy around to the back."

After helping Hunter carefully load the backseat of the buggy, Faith watched him pull down the lane. *Business partners.* The words carried a different meaning from *business associates*, and Faith liked the idea of partnering with Hunter to meet her goal. She might never have the support of a husband, but at least for the moment she had a kind man to encourage her and give her a hand when she needed his help. And, she had to admit, she secretly felt complimented that this kind man happened to have referred to her as a "becoming woman," too.

As his horse galloped toward Piney Hill, Hunter's mood was buoyant, knowing he was helping Faith try to meet her financial obligations while simultaneously meeting his own. He recalled how her countenance shone while they discussed ways to increase revenue, and it was a boost to his confidence that she clearly valued his input. Grateful he could apply the accounting skills he was learning at the cannery to Faith's books, Hunter hoped the experience might allow him to earn a living in Indiana doing something other than the manual labor he'd been accustomed to performing.

Of course, he wasn't yet financially independent by any means: his aunt supplied all of his and his mother's meals and sundries. Ruth insisted, claiming she was beholden to them for looking after *her*. That's why when Hunter first informed his aunt and mother he was going to run Faith's morning deliveries, he didn't care if they exchanged knowing glances. He preferred for them to imagine he was taking on the extra responsibility because he fancied Faith than to realize it was because he'd come perilously close to losing the house in Indiana.

But that danger was behind him for the time being. According to his calculations, with the money he'd earn from the deliveries, plus the fee James Palmer would pay when he picked up the finished chair on Monday, Hunter not only would be able to pay the outstanding house and medical bills, he might have enough left over to purchase a small Christmas gift for his aunt and mother. His breath formed steam in the frosty morning air as he called out to God, *"Denki, Lord, for Your plentiful blessings!"*

He made good time getting to the festival, and the printing shop had just opened when he pulled into the parking lot on his return trip. The manager offered to print the labels within half an hour, but Hunter didn't want to risk returning late to the cannery, so he agreed to pick them up the following morning.

After returning from Piney Hill, Hunter brought the horse and buggy home and then walked back into town. If his hips and legs felt clunky, the sensation was negligible compared with the feelings of competence and optimism carrying him down Main Street and into the cannery.

Maybe it's not so unreasonable to believe I'll be able to support a wife and family one day soon, he allowed himself to think as he gazed out the window while waiting for Ivy to arrive. Spotting Faith's quick, energetic movements in the storefront of her bakery, he again pondered why she wasn't being courted. Faith was so clever, persevering and vivacious. She was someone who seemed to really love to laugh... most of the time. What was the secret burden she hid beneath her quick smile? Hunter had no idea, but whatever it was, he doubted it was the reason she wasn't being courted. More likely, she had no interest in marriage because she was consumed with her business. Didn't she say the bakery was her future?

Ivy passed by the cannery window and lifted her hand toward the bakery storefront, startling Hunter from his thoughts. Flipping the door sign, he greeted her when she came in.

"Hunter Schwartz had Thanksgiving dinner with Faith Yoder on Thursday at Ruth Graber's house. One thirty," Ivy stated as she turned a jar of preserves so its label was aligned with the others.

"*Jah*, that's right. You were there, too, with your *groossdaadi*," Hunter acknowledged. "I enjoyed myself very much, did you?"

"*Jah*, I enjoyed myself very much," she repeated. "A special occasion."

Hunter barely had time to grin back at the winsome young girl before the first of a long stream of customers entered the shop. Sales didn't slow down until right before Hunter closed the store at five o'clock. As he meandered home, he noticed snowflakes that were so light they appeared to be floating upward instead of falling down. He'd felt his legs and hips growing tighter throughout the day, but the store was bustling and he hadn't wanted to retreat to the back room to stretch. Now, the cold air worked its way into his joints, and with each footfall he imagined his legs cracking like ice. Once home, he declined supper, opting for a hot bath. He was asleep within minutes of lying down, and it seemed within minutes of sleeping, it was time for him to rise again.

Although his back was still stiff and the short buggy ride into town the next morning seemed to rattle his bones, all discomfort was forgotten when Faith unlocked the back door for him. Her smile was a sunrise as she extended a steaming mug of coffee.

"*Guder mariye*, Hunter."

"*Guder mariye*," he echoed, his fingers momentarily encircling hers as he accepted the hot drink. "I'm glad to see you secured the door today."

"*Jah*, I might be as stubborn as a mule, but may it never be said I'm *foolhardy*." The glimmer in her eyes told him she was jesting at her own expense. There was something fetching about her ability to be lighthearted so early in the morning that lifted Hunter's disposition, too. "Would you like a muffin with your *kaffi*?" she asked.

"*Denki*, I'd appreciate that." Having skipped supper the night before, he was ravenous. "But I'll have to eat it in the buggy. I want to allow time to stop at the printer's on the way back and pick up your labels."

When he arrived at the festival booth, the *Englisch* vendor greeted him enthusiastically. "I'm glad to see you brought more items today," she said. "Your goodies sold out by eleven in the morning yesterday. I had several people stop by in the evening who said they'd eaten the cookies during the day at work and wanted to purchase some for their families. Faith ought to increase the volume even more than what I see here. My booth closes at six thirty, but there's a big rush between about four and six o'clock, when people are getting out of work. You could make a second delivery for the late-afternoon shoppers, say, around three thirty? People are always drawn to goodies still warm from the oven."

Hunter couldn't have been more pleased. "That's an interesting proposal. I'll talk to Faith about it."

By the time he picked up the labels, returned home, stabled the horse and walked back to town, Hunter had come up with a plan for how he could make an afternoon delivery in addition to his morning run. But since it was already four minutes before nine o'clock, he decided he'd propose his strategy to Faith during her dinner break.

So, while Pearl and Ivy ate their meals at a table in the front of the bakery, Hunter quietly repeated the vendor's suggestion to Faith in the back room. "If you'd like me to make a second daily delivery, I figured out how to make it work. Ivy and Pearl could switch places in the afternoon. That way, Pearl would be available to help you with the extra baking for most of the day, but I wouldn't have to leave Ivy unattended to make an afternoon delivery."

"I don't know…" Faith wrung her hands.

"If you're hesitant about working with Ivy, you needn't be. She's very diligent. I realize she doesn't like making changes, but she's so fond of you I think she'd flourish here. And I can't imagine Pearl objecting." Hunter had to pause to catch his breath. "I truly believe this will put you in a much better position to make your down payment."

"Well, then, let's do it!" Faith exclaimed loudly, smiling so broadly her ears wiggled. "Of course, we'll have to ask Pearl and Ivy first."

"Ask us what?" Pearl called from the other room.

Faith and Hunter charged into the storefront, both speaking so excitedly they kept interrupting each other as they asked Pearl and Ivy to participate in their plan.

"I think it's a splendid idea," Pearl said. "What do you think, Ivy?"

"I'll work in Faith Yoder's bakery from three

o'clock until five o'clock," Ivy agreed. "A splendid idea."

Hunter felt like hugging the girl. Instead, he silently thanked the Lord for how smoothly the plan was coming together. When he told Ruth about it, she was thrilled, too.

"I've been concerned Ivy isn't being challenged enough in the cannery. A change will do her good. But it's a waste of time for you to return home to fetch the buggy twice a day. It would be better to hitch the horse in town. You can take breaks to feed and water him there."

"Are you sure?" Hunter asked. His frame was already aching from a single jaunt into town and he imagined it would only worsen when he began doubling his trips.

"I'm sure. It's not as if your *mamm* and I need the buggy ourselves," Ruth said. "I hope this plan pays off. I know how much Faith's bakery means to her."

Indeed, the first week of delivering baked goods twice daily to the festival proved even more lucrative than Hunter expected, benefiting them both, and Ivy adapted quickly to her new afternoon role at the bakery. All around, Hunter's new partnership with Faith was what the *Englisch* referred to as a win-win situation. Or, as he preferred to think of it, an answer to prayer.

Chapter Seven

◁~◁

Faith yawned as she locked the front door to the bakery after Ivy left for the evening on Monday. For a week, Faith had been arriving ninety minutes earlier to keep up with baking for the in-store sales and her customers' special orders, as well as for the festival. She figured Henrietta couldn't fault her for not spending more time with her family in the morning, since everyone was still sleeping when she left for the bakery anyway. She tried to get home in time to help prepare supper, but there were some evenings, like tonight, when she had to stay late to clean the pans and utensils she didn't have time to wash during the day.

She was rinsing the trays when someone rapped on the pane of the front door. A woman dressed in hospital scrubs cupped her hands against the glass and peered in, while a second woman continued knocking.

"Oh, thank you!" the first woman, a blonde, exclaimed when Faith opened the door. "We were afraid we missed you."

Faith regretted turning away customers, even after hours, but her shelves were nearly bare. "I'm sorry, but the bakery is actually closed and I'm sold out of almost everything," she said.

"I'm not surprised," the blonde replied. "We purchased one of your sticky bun wreaths at the festival on our way to work today, and it was so fantastic we wanted to come by on our way home to see what else you make. We'd like to place a large order for brunch on Friday."

"Yeah," the other woman added, "your husband suggested we give you a call, but we wanted to sample a few items before deciding what to get."

"My husband?" Faith echoed. "I don't have a husband."

The first woman replied, "The man making deliveries isn't your husband? Sorry, he raved so much about you I just assumed you were newlyweds."

Faith felt as if her skin burst into flame. Waving her hand dismissively, she said, "Ah, well, you know how men enjoy food. They're very complimentary when it comes to a woman's baking."

"It wasn't just your baking he complimented," the woman insisted. "What was it he said when he was giving us directions, Rita?"

The other woman sighed theatrically. "He said there may be several businesses with the name 'Yoder's' in Lancaster County, but we'd know we were in the right shop if the owner had hair the color of ground cinnamon and a *wunderbaar* laugh."

Faith's knees felt wiggly. Did Hunter really say that? She invited the women inside and served them samples of the freshest items still in stock. After helping them decide what to order for their party and sending them off with a complimentary loaf of bread that would have wound up in her brothers' bellies, she returned to her dishwashing task.

Denki, Lord, that everything seems to be working out, Faith prayed as she slid a tray into the rack to dry. Her cookies, breads and pastries were selling out daily at the festival. Meanwhile, Pearl and Ivy had adjusted well to the changes; Pearl claimed she preferred the relatively slower afternoons in the cannery, whereas Ivy was flourishing in her new role at the bakery.

What especially gladdened Faith was seeing Hunter's face first thing in the morning. No matter how early the hour or biting the air, he always wore a dashing grin and he was appreciative of the coffee she prepared for him to take on his deliveries. One morning she even convinced him to sit down for a breakfast of French toast topped with pecans, since she knew how much he liked them. Other than Pearl, she'd never had someone express such an active interest in the success of her business, and she wanted him to know she appreciated his support. It didn't hurt that she thoroughly enjoyed his company, either.

When Faith finished washing the dishes, she double-checked the storefront and back room for any last-minute tidying. The following day was Tuesday, December 8, and the bakery and cannery would be closed so she, Pearl, Ivy and Hunter could attend Penelope and Lawrence's wedding in Penelope's hometown. The occasion would begin with a three-hour service in the morning, followed by meals and socializing lasting until nine or ten o'clock at night. It was an Amish tradition for businesses—and even schools—to shut down so all the *leit* could attend the weddings of couples in their districts, which were held on Tuesdays or Thursdays during November and December. Confident nothing was left undone, Faith locked the shop and made it home just in time for supper.

"Are you certain you want to charge Penelope for the wedding cakes?" Henrietta asked Faith later that evening while hemming a seam in her son's trousers.

Ever since Willa left, Henrietta seemed more focused on Faith's work at the bakery. She was continually asking Faith about her orders and making suggestions about what Christmas goodies the customers might enjoy. Faith appreciated her interest, but Henrietta couldn't seem to understand that some traditional Amish items, such as skillet pear ginger pie, weren't in demand enough to be worth preparing them.

"Why shouldn't I charge Penelope for the cakes? She's a customer like anyone else."

While Amish weddings often included homemade pies, cakes and goodies prepared by family members and friends, it wasn't unusual for the bride to purchase one or more cakes from a professional baker, too. Although the cakes were plainer than those at most *Englisch* weddings, they were still special-ordered for the occasion.

"*Jah*, but you're friends with the bride and especially the groom," Henrietta argued. "You were walking out with Lawrence, after all."

That's the very reason I shouldn't *bake their cake at no cost*, Faith thought facetiously as she adorned the fireplace mantel with boughs of evergreen and a solitary red candle in the center. Ornate Christmas decorations were prohibited by the *Ordnung*, but simple garnishing was allowed in Amish homes and businesses, and Faith relished creating a festive environment for her family and customers to enjoy at this time of year.

"Reuben is friends with Turner King, but when Reuben's buggy needs repair, Turner doesn't fix it for free," Faith countered, trying to help Henrietta see her decision from a business perspective. "Likewise, Reuben doesn't stock the Masts' pantry with free produce during harvest season simply because you're friends with Colette."

"*Jah*, but Reuben and Turner are men. Their incomes are necessities—they support their families," Henrietta reasoned.

"My income will allow me to keep the bakery and lease a living space for myself," Faith said as calmly as she could.

"But that's not essential. You could always live here. Either way, a few wedding cakes aren't likely to set you back. It seems you could be a little more gracious to your friends, that's all."

"A little more gracious?" Faith sputtered, twirling toward Henrietta. "Do you have any idea how much graciousness it takes to attend the wedding of a man who rejected me because of something that's not even my fault?"

Her sister-in-law peered at Faith over her reading glasses as if she couldn't quite fathom what was causing her to be so distressed. Faith lowered her volume. She didn't want to speak in anger: she wanted Henrietta to understand how she felt and to stop interfering in her business.

"Listen, Henrietta, not only am I closing the bakery to attend Penelope and Lawrence's wedding—which means I'll lose a full day's worth of business during the busiest season of the year—but as a gift to the couple, I gave Penelope a steep discount. She only paid for whatever ingredients I didn't have in stock, such as coconut milk for the special frosting she requested. So please, show *me* a little graciousness. If you can't support me, at least don't lecture me on how to run my business or conduct my friendships. I know you intend to be helpful, but sometimes your comments are actually quite hurtful."

When Henrietta didn't reply, Faith simply bid her good-night and went upstairs to her room. She had never spoken to her sister-in-law so firmly, but she wasn't going to apologize. Not tonight, anyway. Too tired to undress, she unlaced her boots and collapsed into bed, pulling the quilt over her sideways. Covering her head with her arm, she nestled into her pillow and before she knew it, her nephew was jostling her awake.

"*Mamm* said I'm not to bother you, *Ant* Faith,"

the five-year-old announced in a raspy voice. "You need privacy to get ready for your wedding."

Faith groggily opened her eyes to discover she was nose to nose with the chubby youngster. *"Lappich bu,"* she said, affectionately referring to him as a silly boy as she reached out to touch his ruddy cheek. "It's not *my* wedding we're going to."

"Why not?" He tipped his head and squinted. "Don't you want to have a wedding?"

His innocent curiosity caught her off guard, and she tried to distract him by tossing aside the quilt and shifting to a sitting position.

"Not today I don't," she answered succinctly.

"But when you get married, you get your own special cake."

The boy's sentiment caused Faith to burst out in laughter. *"Jah,* that's true, Andy, but when you get married, you're also pleased to share your special cake with your wedding guests. You'll see—today you'll get a slice."

"I will?" His enormous eyes seemed to grow even larger.

"There you are, Andrew," Henrietta called as she peeked around the divider. *"Kumme,* let your *ant* get dressed while I comb your hair."

"Guder mariye, Henrietta," Faith said as she rose, hoping there was no lingering tension be-

tween them. "I must have been more tired than I realized. I rarely sleep past sunrise."

"*Jah*, it's half-past the hour. We'll be leaving in five minutes."

"Five minutes!" Faith shrieked. "I only have five minutes to get ready?"

Henrietta flinched as if she'd been hurt. "I thought you were waiting to get up and get ready until we were all out of your way and you could have the washroom to yourself. I was trying not to interfere. I assumed Hunter would be picking you up shortly after we left."

Although she believed Henrietta had her best intentions at heart, Faith was too dismayed about being late to mince words. "I don't know how many times I have to tell you I'm not romantically involved with Hunter Schwartz," Faith said with an emphasis she hoped was convincing, "And he is not picking me up, so I'll need to go with you and Reuben and the *kinner*."

She grabbed a pair of stockings from her drawer, whisked her clean dress from the closet and then hurried down the hall to the washroom to try to make herself appear more presentable on the outside than she felt on the inside.

Hunter shifted on the long, hard bench. He felt as fidgety as a child, but he couldn't sit still; the knot of pain in his lower back and hips was radiating downward, causing his left foot to tingle. He'd noticed his discomfort grew progressively worse ever since he began the afternoon deliveries, and he regretted making the long journey to Penelope's house on the one day he could have had a respite from traveling in the buggy. But Ruth had come down with a bad cold and she insisted he attend to extend her good wishes to the young couple. His mother stayed behind, too.

If there was one consolation, it was that the wedding allowed Hunter the opportunity to socialize with Faith. Over the past week, he'd enjoyed bantering with her first thing in the morning before he headed to Piney Hill, or lingering over a treat in the back room of the bakery before he left for the festival in the afternoon. But their visits were always briefer than he would have preferred and their conversations were usually focused on their businesses. He was hoping the late-afternoon wedding festivities would include the kind of fun and games he'd engaged in with Faith and her brothers when he took her home after Thanksgiving dinner.

By the time the three-hour service ended, Hunter could barely pull himself to his feet. He picked up the wooden bench and stiffly hobbled toward where the men were stacking them so a second group could carry them to the bench wagon. If this were a regular worship service, they'd flip and stack the benches to create tables for the *leit* to gather around to eat dinner. But since it was a wedding, the guests would eat in shifts at special tables the men were setting up in a U shape around the gathering room.

Hunter hoped no one noticed how haltingly he moved, and as soon as the men's work was finished, he slipped outside to pace around the yard, hoping to loosen his muscles before it was his turn to sit down to eat. The wind was raw, and he rubbed his hands together. On his third loop around the perimeter, a small child came bounding across the yard.

"Andy!" he heard a female beckon remotely. "Andy, you stop wherever you are right now. This isn't a game. We're not playing tag!"

The child giggled and continued to run pell-mell toward where Hunter was standing. Despite the ache in his lower body, Hunter bent over and adroitly scooped the boy up, somersaulting him into a sitting position on his right shoulder. A moment later, Faith appeared from around the side of the large house. Her shawl was askew and her cheeks were aflame, whether from the cold or from emotion, Hunter didn't know.

"Is this the runaway you're looking for?" he

asked as he flipped Andy upside down and set him back on his feet.

"*Jah*, this is my nephew Andy," she panted. "Andy, say hello to Hunter."

Andy looked up in awe at Hunter. "You're even stronger than my *daed*!" he declared.

Chuckling, Hunter replied, "I'm not sure about that. But what I do know is if you keep eating all of the meat and vegetables your *mamm* serves you, you'll grow to be big and strong like your *daed*, too."

"I always clean my plate," Andy happily informed him. "Especially today. Today we get to have wedding cake after dinner."

"I'm looking forward to that," Hunter commented. "I heard your *ant* Faith made it, and everything she bakes is *appenditlich*."

"*Jah*, but it's not her wedding cake. It's for Penelope and Lawrence. They have to share," Andy carefully explained. "Ant Faith doesn't want to get married. She told *mamm* she's not 'mantically interested in—"

"Look!" Faith interrupted, taking Andy by the hand. "Here comes your *daed*. He's been searching for you."

As Reuben approached the trio, Andy ducked behind Faith's skirt.

"There's no use hiding, Andy," Reuben scolded. "You've already been disobedient, running away like you did. I'm afraid there will be no wedding cake for you."

The boy's eyes immediately welled but he nodded sadly, as if to accept his punishment.

"He gave us a fright when we couldn't find him, it's true," Faith intervened. "But I don't think he meant to. I think he was stretching his legs after sitting so still through the entire service. I'm sure he won't run away again, will you, Andy?"

"No, never," Andy agreed. "I'm sorry I gave you a fright, *Daed*."

Reuben paused before tousling the boy's hair. "You're forgiven, *suh*. I suppose your running about like that made you extra hungry, so you may have a piece of wedding cake after all. *Kumme*, let's go back inside."

Faith and Andy led the way, with Hunter and Reuben following. As they walked toward the house, Reuben confided, "One of the challenges of being a *daed* is knowing when to show grace and when to stand firm for the *kinner's* sake."

"It seems today you've made the right decision," Hunter responded.

"The doubts linger," Reuben replied. "If you have *kinner* one day, you'll know what I mean. Being a *daed* is difficult work."

Hunter thought of the grace and forgiveness his father had shown him throughout his life.

Considering his own behavior, especially during his *Rumspringa* years, he knew it must not have always been easy for his father, and suddenly a great loneliness washed over him.

"Being a *daed* is definitely a weighty responsibility," he affirmed. Then, remembering what his father said to him right before he died, he added, "But I'm told it's one of life's greatest blessings."

"No doubt about that," Reuben agreed.

Faith felt like crying. It wasn't that she had any abiding heartache because Lawrence rejected her and married Penelope. Nor was it because, halfway through the sermon, Faith realized in her haste to get ready, she'd grabbed her baking apron instead of a clean one to wear over her dress. As disheveled as she felt, that wasn't nearly enough to reduce her to tears, either. Nor did she cry out when Andy accidentally hopped on her big toe with the heel of his boot right before he took off across the lawn.

No, it was Hunter's statement about fatherhood being a blessing unlike any other that crushed her spirit. Until she heard him make that comment, Faith hadn't realized the extent of her affection for him. Without fully being aware of it, she must have allowed Henrietta's fanciful imaginings about their walking out together go to her head, because lately Faith had been entertaining notions that perhaps, just perhaps, her relationship with Hunter might develop from that of business partners and friends into a more personal connection.

But what sense was there in daydreaming about a romance with Hunter when he hadn't given the slightest indication he was interested in courting her? As she'd explained to Willa, Hunter was only in Willow Creek temporarily until Ruth's fractures healed. Even if Willa was right and Hunter developed a reason to settle in Pennsylvania permanently, Faith couldn't consider him as a suitor, knowing what she did about her health condition. Hunter made it clear long ago that he wouldn't court anyone he didn't intend to marry. And now, Hunter made it clear he wanted children, too. Why wouldn't he want them? It was only natural; Faith couldn't fault him for that. But neither could she continue to kid herself: Hunter was helping her save her business and that was all. She needed to squelch her unrealistic romantic yearnings.

But that was easier said than done when she was surrounded by people extolling the virtues of marriage. She was as sociable and courteous as she could be, but after several hours her cheeks ached from plastering a smile across her face. Seeking to leave with Henrietta and Reuben when they took the boys home, she poked her head into the kitchen in search of her sister-in-law.

"Faith, those cakes you made are as scrumptious as they are beautiful," Doris Plank gushed. "You have a real talent."

"Denki," Faith replied, relieved that everyone seemed to be enjoying her confections.

"Don't you worry, your turn will come soon enough," Doris continued. "Look at me—I was well into my thirties when I married, and now here I am with a *bobbel* in my arms! You've got plenty of time, doesn't she, Collette?"

"Jah," replied Collette Mast, one of Henrietta's friends. "Your sister-in-law frets about your future, but I tell her anyone who can bake like you do will make an excellent wife."

Mortified that Henrietta had been discussing her fears about Faith's lack of suitors with Collette Mast, Faith quickly excused herself and walked outside toward the barn where the other single people were gathering before the second meal. It was an Amish tradition for the bride and groom or another married couple to pair young male guests with young female guests. The couples were expected to sit together and converse during the informal supper that occurred in the early evening. As she wove through the crowd, Faith spotted Mason speaking with Katie Fisher, so she asked him if he'd seen Reuben, Henrietta and the children.

"They already left," Mason told her. "Henrietta suggested you might like to stay and socialize, since you've been working such long hours. I told her you could ride with Katie and me if no one else offers to take you home. But Penelope's already started the matchmaking, so perhaps she'll pair you with someone who has a courting buggy."

Faith rubbed her forehead in disgrace. Her brother's halfhearted offer of transportation home was embarrassing enough, but now she'd also have to endure the humiliation of Lawrence's bride matching her with a man she deemed suitable? Faith silently considered walking to the nearest phone shanty and calling a cab. It would almost be worth the expense.

"What your brother means to say is any man would be privileged to give you a ride home, Faith," Katie tactfully clarified, elbowing Mason. "But if not, we'd *wilkom* your company."

As it turned out, Penelope paired Faith with Hunter, the one man she was specifically trying to avoid. They took seats opposite one another at the far end of the table. The room was filled with noisy chatter, so when Hunter spoke, Faith had to ask him to repeat himself.

Rather than raising the volume of his voice, he leaned forward to be heard.

"I said you look a bit drawn. Have you been eating enough?"

No one had ever asked her that question before, and she couldn't tell if he was joking.

"I haven't *stopped* eating," she said, gesturing to the plate piled with macaroni and cheese, fried sweet potatoes and chicken.

"There sure are plenty of tasty dishes to choose from," Hunter remarked. "And I heard everyone praising the wedding cake you made."

"Almost everyone—Andy was disappointed. He complained it wasn't nearly as *gut* as one of my peanut butter sheet cakes." Faith giggled, relaxing a little. "I told him when he's old enough to marry, that's what kind I'll make for him."

Hunter flashed a broad smile. "You have a special way with *kinner.*"

Faith had heard this compliment before, and it was often followed by a remark about how she'd make a terrific mother someday. Because motherhood was most definitely not a topic she cared to discuss with Hunter, she simply shrugged and said, "He's my nephew, so I'm used to handling his behaviors."

"Neh," Hunter protested. "It's not just with your nephew. It was also with Ivy at the bridge. You were so nurturing and calm—"

Growing more defensive, Faith snapped, "Ivy's a young woman, not a *kind*. I knew what to say to her because the situation happened many times before, not because of any inherent maternal instinct on my part."

As she straightened her posture, she realized she'd been leaning so far forward that a glob of macaroni and cheese had gotten stuck to the front of her cape. Inwardly and outwardly, she couldn't have felt any less attractive than she did at that moment.

Hunter swallowed. He hadn't meant to insult Ivy; he only meant to pay Faith a compliment. She was usually so good-humored and easy to talk to, yet as he watched her bowing her head to wipe the front of her cape with a napkin, he realized she was in pain. It wasn't necessarily physical pain that disturbed her, but she was undeniably deeply troubled. He recognized the symptoms. After all, how many times had he forced himself to put on a good face—or at least go through the motions of what was expected of him—when inwardly, he was grimacing in agony?

After a brief silence, he apologized. "I'm sorry. I know Ivy isn't a *kind*, and I don't think I've ever treated her like one. I have nothing but respect for her diligence and gratitude for her skills. I'd be lost without her at the cannery. I only meant you seem to know the right thing to say at the right time to keep a situation from growing worse."

Faith placed her napkin beside her plate. "You needn't apologize, Hunter," she said. "Once again, I'm the one who ought to be sorry. I'm afraid I'm not much of a supper companion. If you'll excuse me, I need some air."

After hurriedly sopping up the last of his gravy with his bread crust, Hunter followed Faith outdoors. He passed several young couples exchanging sweet nothings in hushed tones near the side of the house. If he knew Faith, she'd seclude herself on the farthest end of the property, much like she'd done at the creek at her house the Sunday the Yoders hosted church. Squinting, he carefully picked his way across the property.

"You haven't got on a shawl," he said when he spied her leaning against a willow tree.

"You aren't wearing a coat," she countered.

"I'm too full to be cold."

Her laughter sounded the way the stars looked in the night sky: clear and bright. "That doesn't make any sense," she scoffed lightly.

"It doesn't make any sense to leave the table before dessert is served, either, but here you are," he replied.

"I'll hardly starve."

"But you'll miss the best part of the meal," Hunter objected. When his comment elicited only a shrug from Faith, he realized he was being dense. "Ach! I understand. You didn't want to be paired with me."

"Neh," she said. "I mean, it's not that I didn't want to be paired with you, Hunter. It's that I didn't want to be paired with anyone. I wanted to go home hours ago, which I know seems like an ungracious thing to say, but I just feel… I feel so…"

"You feel so what?" He noticed she had a tendency to withhold her thoughts, but he hoped she was becoming more comfortable expressing herself to him. Trying to draw her out, he teased, "You're not coming down with something, are you?"

"Neh, it's not that." Faith strolled a few yards from the tree, keeping her back turned toward Hunter as she continued to explain. "I used to walk out with Lawrence until…until he decided he didn't want to marry me. It was a very difficult time, but now I wish him and Penelope all the best, I truly do… I just wish I didn't have to wish it all day long, if that makes sense."

Because he recalled how relieved he was not to be present in Indiana to attend Justine's wedding, Hunter understood perfectly. For the life of him, though, he couldn't imagine why Lawrence would choose a girl like Penelope over a woman like Faith. Hunter thought about little Andy saying Faith didn't want to marry. Was her heartache over Lawrence what made her decide she was no longer interested in marriage to any man?

"I can't say I blame you for wanting to leave," he admitted. "If you wouldn't object to being paired with me for the journey home, I'm happy to take you now."

"Really?" Faith questioned. "You're sure you're ready to go, too?"

"I'm sure," Hunter replied.

Faith's company was the only reason he'd stayed so late, and now that he knew she preferred to leave, there was no sense in his sticking around, either. He'd much rather share three minutes of genuine, joyful interaction with Faith at the bakery than three hours of contrived, cheerless courtship at a social event—even if he was the one who specifically requested Penelope match him with Faith in the first place.

Chapter Eight

As grateful as Faith was to Hunter for helping her depart the celebration prematurely, she was simultaneously dismayed at herself for divulging the reason she wanted to escape. *What a bobblemoul I am*, she thought, *blabbering on about Lawrence like that*. Hunter characteristically was an attentive and nonjudgmental listener, but he wasn't Faith's confidant, and she was mortified that she disclosed such personal feelings. If she wasn't more careful, who knows what else she'd share in a moment of emotional distress? She resolved to keep her mouth shut on the way home, but as it happened, Hunter barely uttered a word, either.

Because she accepted a ride with him instead of returning home with Mason after the wedding, Faith knew there'd be no convincing her sister-in-law she wasn't walking out with

Hunter, so she decided she wouldn't try. When she entered her room, she simply greeted Henrietta, who was tucking the boys in for the night.

"I'm tired. I think I'll go to bed now, too," she whispered. *"Gut nacht."*

Yet instead of sleeping, she interlaced her fingers behind her head and stared at the ceiling.

"Ant Faith," her nephew whispered from the other side of the divider, interrupting her thoughts. "Are you awake?"

"Jah, what is it, Andy?"

"Mamm says soon you're going to leave us to go live in the bakery."

"Jah, in an apartment above the bakery."

"Don't you like living with us anymore?"

"Of course I do. But when I move to the apartment above the bakery, your *daed* can take the divider down and you and your brother will have lots more space."

"I don't want lots more space." Andrew sniffed. "I want you to stay here with us."

Faith squeezed her eyes tightly, and two tears dribbled down each side of her face. "I will visit every Sunday, and you may visit me above the bakery, too."

"Will your compartment smell like peanut butter sheet cake?"

Faith giggled. *"Jah*, I suppose my *apart*ment will smell like peanut butter sheet cake if that's what I've made in the bakery. When you visit, we'll eat a piece of whatever I baked that day, okay?"

"I would like that, *Ant* Faith. *Gut nacht*," the boy whispered sleepily.

"Gut nacht."

As Faith stretched on her bed, she was filled with self-doubt. Maybe her sister-in-law was right: it wasn't essential for her to move or even for her to earn a salary—Henrietta probably would have been more appreciative of Faith's help at home, in the garden and around the farm than she was of the financial contributions Faith made toward their household expenses.

Faith asked herself why she was striving so hard for something that wasn't considered a necessity. She already knew the answer: she liked being a business owner, she liked serving her customers and she liked baking. There was nothing she was better at doing or relished doing more.

In fact, for the first time since Lawrence broke up with her, Faith realized how relieved she was that she hadn't end up marrying him after all. She'd been a farmer's daughter her entire youth. She'd had a wonderful childhood and learned many useful skills, but she didn't necessarily want to be a farmer's wife—or a farmer's sister, for that matter—and spend the rest of her life on a farm. Was it so wrong to want to do something different, since she had a choice?

She wished Henrietta and other women in her district understood that just because she was a single woman didn't mean her business was a mere hobby to distract her until she got married. Granted, virtually all Amish women quit working full-time once they had children, so she could see why some people assumed the bakery was only a passing interest, but Henrietta knew better. She knew Faith might never marry or have children. Faith resented that her sister-in-law didn't seem to accept that Faith's life was following a course that was different from Henrietta's.

Faith shifted onto her side, cocooning herself in the quilt. Even Hunter's observation, "you have a special way with *kinner*," seemed fraught with the underlying expectation she would eventually nurture children of her own. Or was she reading too much into his praise? Had seeing Lawrence again influenced her perception, causing her to feel as if she couldn't quite measure up to anyone's standards? She didn't know what to think anymore.

All that was certain was she had three weeks to meet her financial goal and she wasn't going to let anything stop her from doing her best to raise the money she needed. Slipping an arm from beneath her covers, she pulled her battery-operated alarm clock from her nightstand, set it to three thirty and placed it beside her on the pillow. Three thirty was a ridiculously early hour to rise, but how else could she keep up with the orders and in-shop sales? She couldn't risk falling behind, not with her deadline only weeks away.

The next morning there was a thin sheet of ice on the road, and twice the bicycle almost skidded out from under her, but she pedaled as quickly as she could. On the way, she determined she had set a poor precedent by chatting with Hunter each morning and afternoon. By doing so, she had allowed herself to imagine a flirtation existed between them. Further, those precious minutes were better spent kneading dough, mixing ingredients or otherwise preparing the bakery to receive customers. She also decided she and Pearl needn't be so chatty: they could increase their productivity if they spent less time jabbering and more time baking.

As efficient as Ivy was at boxing the customers' selections for them, Faith still had to be present to ring up their purchases, which disrupted her afternoon baking. Recalling that Hunter told her Ruth thought Ivy needed more challenges, Faith wondered if she could assign Ivy some light baking responsibilities. She expected since Ivy was excellent with numbers, she'd have no problem with measurements and following the sequence of a recipe, once she committed it to memory. It was worth a try.

By the time she arrived at the bakery, Faith was trembling with cold and excitement. The wedding was behind her: this was a new day and a fresh opportunity to apply herself to the undertaking that would bring her far greater contentment than if she had married Lawrence. She was certain of it.

A week after the wedding, Hunter crept up the back steps to the bakery, pausing before he rapped on the door. After each delivery, his legs, hips and back ached with an intensity he hadn't experienced since immediately following the accident. The night before, he'd suffered through a particularly sleepless night, and his left leg was buzzing with pain.

"*Guder mariye*, Pearl," he said when the elder woman opened the door. "I didn't expect to see you here already."

"Faith asked me to arrive early. She wants— I mean, *we* want—to increase the festival sales even more," Pearl explained, wiping the back of her hand across her brow.

"If you don't mind my saying so, Pearl, you

look as if you could use a cup of *kaffi*," Hunter hinted. "I know I could."

Faith bustled into the room from the storefront. "I thought I heard you gabbing with someone," she said to Pearl. "*Guder mariye*, Hunter."

"We were hardly gabbing," Pearl replied, clearly bristling. "We were just commenting about how we need a cup of *kaffi*. I'll put a pot on."

"But that will take—"

"It will only take a few minutes," Pearl interrupted. "And while it's brewing, I'll wrap the last of the gingerbread cookies—rather, the gingerbread *men* for Hunter to take with him."

Ever since the wedding, Hunter sensed Faith was rushing him out the door. Gone was her customary smile and garrulous greeting. Instead, she barely glanced up long enough to load his arms with stacks of boxed goodies. At first, he wondered if he'd done something to offend her, but now that he observed how blunt she was being with Pearl, he realized it was more likely she was tense about her looming financial deadline. Realizing Faith was trying to be as efficient as possible, Hunter suddenly wished he hadn't indicated he wanted coffee. He would have preferred getting on the road to staying in the high-tension environment, especially when he was already on edge from his physical condition.

"Pearl thinks I shouldn't have changed the gingerbread cookies' shapes from circles into gingerbread men," Faith explained, rapidly tying a clear plastic bag with a bright red ribbon. She held it up, displaying its contents: half a dozen gingerbread men, each with white frosting squiggles on their arms and legs, three red dots for buttons, a green bow tie and a smiley face with two eyes. "Although the *Ordnung* doesn't forbid them, Pearl thinks they look like graven images."

"That's not what I said," Pearl clarified. "I said I wouldn't want the *Englisch* to *think* they look like graven images and accuse us of hypocrisy just to sell cookies, since they know we don't allow our *kinner* to own dolls with faces."

Feeling as if his lower back were being prodded with a burning poker, Hunter shifted his stance. "Either way, I'm sure they taste the same," he said diplomatically.

"That's just it—they don't taste the same," Pearl contended. "The round ones are softer. The flatter gingerbread men go brittle enough to crack your teeth in a day."

"Ha!" scoffed Faith. "She's exaggerating. Besides, we make these fresh every morning. It's not our business if the customers keep them in their cupboards for a week. Don't you think the cookies will sell better if they look a bit more festive, Hunter?"

"Er," he stammered. This argument was between Pearl and Faith and he didn't want to give his opinion on the topic, but since Faith pressed him, he answered, "They've sold out nearly every day as they were, so…"

"That's exactly what I said!" Pearl tossed her hands in the air.

"*Jah*, but this way, we'll sell even more of them, which is why I've doubled the amount I'm sending with you, Hunter. They're bigger, so I'm increasing the price, too," Faith reasoned. "But you'll have to be extra careful transporting them, so their arms and legs don't break off."

"Yet another reason the round cookies are more practical," Pearl mumbled as she handed Hunter his coffee.

"*Denki,*" he quietly thanked her.

"Here, let me carry some of these boxes to the buggy," Faith offered, hinting he should be on his way.

"*Neh*, I'll make a couple trips. I don't want to take you away from your baking." Hunter winced as he took a few steps toward the boxes.

"I'll help you," Pearl insisted, and the look on her face indicated neither Faith nor Hunter should challenge her offer.

When they were outside, Pearl questioned whether he was feeling alright. "Your posture seems a little…a little crooked," she noticed.

"I must have slept funny last night," he said.

"You'd better turn in early tonight, then," Pearl lectured kindly. "I'm only now experiencing how imperative it is to get a *gut* night's rest. I'm afraid I'm in a miserable mood without it—and so is our friend Faith."

Despite how uncharacteristically gruff Faith had been, Hunter defended her. "She does seem high-strung, but I imagine she's preoccupied with making the lease down payment."

In the light cast by the open bakery door, Hunter noticed Pearl was arching her eyebrow curiously at him. "That's probably true," she said. "She's blessed to have a young man like you to support her."

I'd do almost anything for Faith. The thought instantly flitted through Hunter's mind, but he couldn't let Pearl assume his support was based on anything other than a business partnership.

"I know she feels blessed to have such a loyal friend and staff member as you, too," he replied. "As for me, I'm glad to have the extra work and she pays me well, but I'd better get going before she changes her mind."

"Be careful," Pearl cautioned. "The roads are

slick, and the *Englisch* aren't always aware of the black ice."

Hunter nodded. "I'll see you in the afternoon."

By the time Ivy and Pearl switched stores at three o'clock, Pearl's energy seemed to have returned. Hunter's, however, was flagging. The pain in his back was so exacting it took all of his stamina simply to place one foot in front of the other to limp down Main Street to the hitching post to retrieve his horse and buggy.

"Hunter!" Faith cheered when he shuffled through the back entrance. "Guess what? Marianne Palmer is having an impromptu neighborhood party and she's asked me to bake pear cake and plum pudding. She's also purchasing six dozen of the gingerbread men for all the *kinner*!"

"That's *wunderbaar*," he acknowledged.

"*Jah*, but there's one little catch. The party is tonight and she asked if we could deliver the goodies to her house since she has to do some last-minute decorating and her husband is out of town. I told her I'd check with you first. After you return from the festival, could you make a second delivery of the cakes? You'd receive double pay, of course."

Hunter's back was causing him such agony that the extra salary held little appeal; all he wanted was to get home and soak in a hot bath. But when he saw the hopeful look in Faith's sparkling eyes, he couldn't say no.

"*Jah*, I'll stop in for Marianne's goods when I get back from Piney Hill," he promised.

Faith didn't tell Hunter she'd already prepared the cakes and begun steaming the puddings for Marianne. It was a risk, but Faith knew she could count on Hunter. She figured if he couldn't make the delivery for some reason, she'd negotiate another arrangement, since she speculated if Marianne was pressed, the woman would find a way to pick up her items in person. If Marianne refused, Faith would have had no choice but to add them to the display case for other customers to buy. But thanks to Hunter's dependability, it hadn't come to that.

With Marianne's order tended to, Faith slid an applesauce cake into the oven. Then, while Ivy helped the steady stream of customers make selections and boxed their goodies for them, Faith devoted herself to ringing up their purchases. After half an hour or so, there was enough of a lull for Faith to lay out the ingredients for Ivy to begin making gingerbread cookies. Since Ivy struggled with manual dexterity, Faith would have to assist when it came time to use the cookie cutter, but Faith figured it would be helpful if Ivy got a start on the dough. She had just finished reviewing the instructions with her when the bell on the front door jangled.

"*Guder nammidaag*, Faith," Isaac Miller greeted her. "I don't see any bread on the shelves, which means you must be holding some for me in the back."

As a widowed man with three small children, Isaac was one of the few Amish customers who depended on Faith's bakery for his bread supply. He stopped in at the end of the day on Tuesdays, Thursdays and Saturdays to purchase two or three loaves of bread. If Faith or Pearl noticed they were running low or Isaac was later than usual, they set a couple of loaves aside for him. But today had been so busy and Faith was distracted by Marianne's last-minute order.

"Ach! I'm sorry, Isaac," she apologized. "I got so caught up in my *Grischtdaag* orders, I entirely forgot."

"Your *Grischtdaag* orders?" Isaac repeated blankly.

Faith was embarrassed, knowing how weak her excuse sounded to an Amish man with three hungry children to feed.

"I'm sorry, Isaac. Let me at least wrap some gingerbread cookies for the *kinner*—no charge," she offered.

"*Neh*. I'd prefer they didn't have sweets today,

since I'll have to stop at the *Englisch* grocery store for bread and that has enough sugar in it to last them a week."

"Oh, okay," Faith uttered. "See you on Saturday, then."

Isaac lifted his hand in a halfhearted wave. No sooner had the door shut behind him than Ivy's piercing wail sounded from the kitchen, followed by a terrible racket.

The puddings! Faith panicked.

But no, Ivy was standing near the open oven, not by the pudding molds. At her feet, the large applesauce cake Faith had been baking was overturned, and a dishcloth lay next to the crumbly mess. Tears streamed down the girl's face as the timer on the back of the oven buzzed loudly.

Faith gasped. "Ivy, are you alright? What happened?"

Ivy pulled away, hiding her hand behind her back.

"Did you burn yourself? Let me have a look," Faith insisted.

The girl slowly opened her fist, allowing Faith to examine her skin.

"It doesn't look that bad." Faith sighed. "Let's run it under cold water, shall we?"

"I did it the way you did it," Ivy sobbed.

"When I took the cake out of the oven, I used the dish cloth so I wouldn't burn myself."

"But Ivy, that cloth was wet. You can't use a wet cloth to retrieve a pan from the oven. That's why you burned your hand," Faith explained, a hint of exasperation in her voice.

"I'm sorry!" Ivy howled louder.

Faith pressed her lips together and counted to five. "It's okay, Ivy. You didn't know. It's not your fault. Please stop crying."

She wrapped her arms around her petite friend and hummed a hymn they'd sung together at Thanksgiving. Soon the young woman's sobs turned into sniffles. Finally, Ivy raised her head from Faith's shoulder and stated, "I need to add one-half of a cup of molasses next."

"Okay, Ivy. You finish mixing the cookie ingredients while I sweep up the cake," Faith instructed.

As she bent to clean the floor, Faith mentally calculated how much money the wasted cake would have garnered in sales. She was immediately ashamed of herself, and her hands trembled as she lifted the dustbin. As regrettable as it was the cake had gone to ruin, she was relieved no harm had come to Ivy. Faith hadn't realized how closely Ivy watched her. From now on, she'd have to remember to use pot holders and avoid other shortcuts she took as an experienced baker. And she'd have to limit Ivy's responsibilities to helping customers, even if it meant Faith might fall behind with the baking.

When Ivy left for the evening, Faith sent half a dozen warm gingerbread men cookies with her, saying, "Your *groossdaadi* will be very impressed you made these."

By that time, Faith had placed another applesauce cake in the oven and was carefully crating the plum pudding and pear cakes for Hunter to deliver to the Palmers' house. Usually he was back long before five, and she wondered what was keeping him. The day had been trying enough with Pearl's complaints and Ivy's mishap; the last thing she wanted was for Hunter to be late with the Palmer delivery.

"There you are!" she exclaimed when he knocked on the door several minutes later. "I was beginning to worry you'd changed your mind and decided to head home for the night instead."

"I gave you my word, so here I am," Hunter replied curtly. "Are these the boxes?"

"Jah," Faith acknowledged. She had only been joking, but judging from Hunter's austere demeanor, she sensed she'd offended him. Trying to make up for it, she offered, "Would you like a cup of *kaffi* before you get back in the buggy? I have some sweet rolls—"

"*Neh*, the roads are icy and I've seen several *Englisch* cars spin out. Rush hour is peaking and I want to make this delivery and get home as soon as I can," he said as he lifted a crate.

"Alright, well, you must be very careful," Faith advised as she held the door for him.

"Don't worry, I have a system for stacking these," Hunter said. "Nothing will get ruined or broken along the way."

Faith had been referring to his safety, not to her baked goods, but he was in too much of a hurry for her to elaborate. After he departed, she tarried on the back doorstep, allowing the sleet to pelt her upturned face as she wondered what Henrietta was fixing for supper that night. Ducking into the bakery, she buttered a roll and poured herself a cup of lukewarm coffee before washing the trays and wrapping the baked goods for the next day.

It was nearly seven o'clock by the time Faith began bicycling toward home. Because she'd never replaced it, the battery in her headlamp was completely depleted and the moon was obscured by clouds. The road was so slick she had to keep dismounting to push the heavy bike along the slipperiest stretches of pavement. Faith knew her sister-in-law would have an opinion about her tardiness, but she didn't want to jeopardize her safety by taking unnecessary chances.

Ivy's burn, however slight, served to warn Faith against reckless behavior.

She'd just pushed her bicycle over the crest of a hill when she heard a horse whinnying and shifting its hooves restlessly against the hard pavement. Faith spied the flashers and headlights of a buggy halted on the opposite side of the road, but she didn't see anyone in the front seat. She dropped her bike and darted toward the carriage, thumping on its exterior frame with her gloved hand. "Hello? Hello? Is someone in there?" she questioned.

"Jah," a man groaned. "I'm in the backseat."

Faith's stomach dropped and her legs went squishy. Although the man's voice was distorted by pain, Faith recognized it immediately. "Hunter!" she cried. "It's me, Faith!"

Hunter felt the buggy shift slightly as Faith climbed inside, and the minor movement caused his lower spine to vibrate with pain.

"Please," he pleaded, "Don't jostle me. I'm… I'm injured."

"Where does it hurt? Tell me what happened!" she pleaded. Her voice was above him now, and although he couldn't see her features in the dim light, her tone conveyed both authority and alarm.

Hunter was in too much misery to detail how, on the return trip from Marianne Palmer's, he thought he heard something slide off the seat behind him. Concerned he'd forgotten to bring one of Faith's boxes into the house, he stopped the horse, set the parking brake and reached into the back of the carriage. When he initially failed to locate anything amiss, he stretched farther, triggering a spasm in the small of his back that was so acute he lost his balance and toppled over the seat, knocking the back of his head when he landed faceup on the floor. Wedged there for at least fifteen minutes, he was writhing in agony when Faith happened upon him.

Light-headed, he could only utter, "My back. I fell and hurt my back. I can't feel my leg."

"Are you bleeding?"

"*Neh.* Just in pain."

Hunter could barely make sense of Faith's movements overhead as she bit the tip of her glove and pulled her fingers free. Pressing her bare hand to the side of his face, she murmured, "Cold and clammy." Then she unwound her shawl and spread it over his chest, tucking it in behind his shoulders.

"Don't worry," she consoled him. "I'm going to run to the phone shanty and call an ambulance. I'll be right back."

"*Neh!*" Hunter roared as another wave of pain coursed through his spine. "No ambulance. Too expensive."

"Hunter, don't be *lecherich*!" Faith argued, calling him ridiculous. "You need medical help and you need it now. There's a medical center in Highland Springs—"

Hunter used his free hand to grab her wrist. "No ambulance," he insisted. "You take me. In this weather, it's safer with a horse and buggy. You take me."

"But Hunter—"

"It's quicker. You take me," he demanded, too afflicted to waste his breath with niceties.

"Okay, let go of my arm and I'll take you," she agreed.

"*Denki*, Faith," he said, and after he released her wrist, he broke out in feverish hilarity. "If you think I'm bad off, wait until you see the gingerbread men I landed on."

"Hush now," Faith instructed over her shoulder before calling for the horse to giddyap.

The buggy lurched forward unevenly, sending another jolt of pain through Hunter's body, and he gasped before passing out. When he came to, he could hear pellets of sleet riveting the roof of the buggy as Faith recited the twenty-third Psalm. In his delirium, he thought he might be dying and he worried about who would take care of his mother now—not that he'd done a very good job of fulfilling his father's final request. Remembering his dad's tortured expression as they lay side by side after the accident, Hunter began to sob.

"It's okay, we're almost there," Faith promised from the front seat. "Be strong for a few minutes longer, Hunter. You're going to be alright."

Hardly able to catch his breath, Hunter felt anything but strong, yet just as the pain escalated to a point he thought was beyond what he could endure, Faith announced, "We're here! *Denki*, Lord, *denki*. You made it, Hunter, we're here."

Though his eyes were closed, Hunter sensed the light brightening around him and he heard someone say, "This area is for ambulances only. You have to move your buggy immediately, miss."

"Not until you help my friend," Faith replied. "He's in the back. His leg is numb and I think he might have bumped his head. He's been in and out of consciousness all the way from Willow Creek. You must help him."

The buggy shifted as someone climbed aboard. Hunter squinted to see two men peering down at him.

"What's your name, son? Can you tell us your name?"

"Hunter Schwartz," he answered, tasting blood. In his torment he must have bitten the inside of his cheek.

"Hunter, we're going to get you out of here, but we have to stabilize your neck and back first, so we're going to secure you on a board that will help us carry you. It might be uncomfortable. Can you tell us what happened?"

"I was hit by a truck," he muttered feebly. He meant to convey it was his previous injury that was plaguing him, but he couldn't form the sentence.

"A truck hit you?" the man repeated. "Were you walking or in your buggy when it hit you?"

"Neh, neh." His head felt so fuzzy.

"Hunter? Hunter, stay with me," the man urged him. "How were you injured?"

"My *daed* died," he groaned, trying to make them understand. "Someone has to let my *mamm* know I'm here. If I'm late returning home, she'll worry that…"

But he passed out again before he could finish expressing the dreadful thought.

Chapter Nine

"**W**as there a fatality at the accident scene?" the medic asked as the men lifted the board Hunter was strapped to onto a gurney.

"What?" At the word *fatality*, Faith's heart pummeled her ribs even harder than it had during the harrowing journey to the hospital. "What accident scene?"

"Hunter said he was hit by a truck and his dad died."

"He was injured and his *daed* was killed when a truck struck their buggy, *jah*," Faith answered, following the men as they wheeled the gurney through the automatic doors of the emergency room entrance. "But that happened over a year ago. He must be confused—could it be from knocking his head?"

The two men met each other's eyes without answering her. "Is he on any meds?" one of them asked. "Any painkillers, herbal remedies, anything like that?"

"Why would he already be on painkillers? He just got here."

A nurse intercepted Faith by her shoulders as the medics briskly rolled the stretcher through another set of doors. "I'm afraid you can't go with them. The doctors will take good care of your friend."

"But I need to make sure he—"

"Look, hon, you're dripping wet," the nurse pointed out. "I'm going to get a thermal blanket for you to wrap yourself in and this young man is going to head outside to hitch your horse, right Tyler?"

A man wearing blue cotton scrubs smiled broadly at her. "If your mare is like my grandpa's, she won't like the sound of the ambulances, so I'll find a quiet, dry place to settle her, okay?"

"Jah," Faith agreed distractedly. Thinking aloud, she added, "I should... I should call the phone shanty. Or maybe Joseph Schrock is still at his shop. He usually stays late on Tuesday nights to do his accounting. I should call him so he can tell Hunter's *mamm* Hunter is here in the hospital."

"That's a good idea," the nurse said kindly, leading Faith to a room containing a small sofa, a row of chairs and an end table with a phone. "I'll be right back with the blanket."

"Denki," Faith automatically replied in *Deitsch*.

She dialed Joseph's number, praying, "Please, *Gott*, let him be there," as the phone rang one, two and then three times.

On the fourth ring Joseph picked up and Faith rushed her words so quickly he interrupted her, asking, "Who is this?"

A second time she explained Hunter's predicament. "I don't know what's wrong with him yet, but the nurse said he's in *gut* hands with the doctors, and we know he's in *Gott's* hands, so he's bound to be alright."

Even as Faith spoke, the phone quivered in her grasp. With the exception of when her *mamm* had been in childbirth with her youngest brother, she'd never heard anyone cry out in pain as Hunter had done during their traumatic trip to the medical center. The only thing more disturbing than Hunter's wails puncturing the night air was when he'd fallen silent in the back of the buggy.

"I'll bring Iris to the hospital straightaway," Joseph suggested.

"Would you send someone to my house in the meantime, to let them know I'm alright?" she asked.

"Of course. I'm sure your absence has them very worried."

Faith wasn't as certain. She'd been working late recently; perhaps Henrietta would assume she was still filling orders at the bakery. Suddenly, Faith missed her family so much that she couldn't wait to kiss her nephews' pudgy cheeks and listen to her brothers' animated joshing at the supper table. More than anyone, Faith missed Henrietta, and she longed to confide to her sister-in-law about her grueling journey into Highland Springs.

While Faith didn't know exactly how Hunter had been injured, she surmised he never would have gotten hurt if she hadn't requested him to make a second delivery just to placate Marianne Palmer. As Faith sat in the deserted waiting room, she realized she not only had been pushing herself too hard lately, but she'd been pushing Pearl, Ivy and Hunter, too. She was filled with such regret that she would have begun blubbering on the spot if the nurse hadn't opened the door to deliver the blanket and a cup of hot tea.

"I'll let you know how Hunter is as soon as I hear from the doctors," she promised.

Despite the thermal blanket and warm drink, Faith couldn't shake the chill that permeated her to the core. Shivering, she recalled the alarmed expressions on the medics' faces when she said Hunter was confused. Did they fear he had a concussion? Then she thought about how Hunter had said he couldn't feel his legs—didn't that indicate paralysis? What if his condition was permanent? What if he couldn't walk again? She'd never forgive herself. *Please, Lord, make Hunter well*, she prayed.

Over an hour later, her head was still bowed in prayer when Hunter's mother and Joseph Schrock entered the room. Faith leaped to her feet to embrace Iris, whose eyes were red-rimmed.

"We saw the nurse on the way in," Iris explained. "She told us Hunter is resting comfortably and we can visit him in a few minutes. *Denki* for bringing him here, Faith. Who knows what might have happened if you hadn't come along the road when you did?"

Still feeling guilty about Hunter's injuries, Faith was relieved when Reuben and Mason strode into the room and she didn't have to reply.

"Faith!" they exclaimed in unison and took turns enveloping her in bear hugs.

"Mason found your bike on the side of the road," Reuben explained. "We didn't know what to think, and Henrietta was frantic. When we went to town to look for you, we crossed paths with Joseph, who was heading to Ruth's house to bring Iris the news. Henrietta stayed behind to assist and comfort Ruth, but I think Ruth might be the one comforting Henrietta instead."

As Reuben finished speaking, the nurse pushed the door ajar. "We're keeping Hunter overnight for observation," she said. "The doctor will explain everything, but Hunter is medicated and he needs to sleep, so we have to limit his visitors."

"May I stay the night?" Iris inquired.

"Of course," the nurse said. "But wouldn't you be more rested if you—"

"I'll stay the night," Iris repeated firmly.

"I'd like to stay with you," Faith offered. "If you don't mind."

"I'd appreciate that."

The men quickly made arrangements to take Ruth's buggy to her house and to return in the morning to transport Iris and Hunter home. Joseph promised he'd also stop at Pearl's house and ask her to mind the bakery for Faith the following morning.

"Tell her not to worry about doing any extra baking," Faith requested. "And please ask her to intercept Ivy from the cannery at nine o'clock sharp, otherwise the poor girl will become distraught."

"I'll be sure to pass along the message," Joseph agreed. "If there's anything else I can do to help with the bakery or the cannery, let me know."

"*Denki*, Joseph," Faith said, and then she turned to embrace her brothers. "I appreciate the two of you coming all this way, too. Please tell Henrietta I promise there will be no more late nights for me."

"You did well, Faith," Reuben whispered into her ear, giving her shoulder a squeeze. "You're a brave woman."

But when Faith opened the door to Hunter's room and glimpsed his ashen complexion against the backdrop of needles, wires and monitors, she felt as timid as a child.

Hunter couldn't lift his eyelids. The nurse informed him he might become drowsy from the medication, but he didn't expect to feel this wiped out. As his muscles relaxed, he began to breathe easier, relieved of the anguish he'd endured for the past several hours.

"Hello, I'm Dr. Henderson," the physician at the end of his bed said to whomever just entered the room.

"I'm Iris Schwartz, Hunter's *mamm*," his mother replied. "And this is Faith."

Aha, so Faith must have notified his mother and aunt about his fall. While he was grateful his mother was aware he was alright, he wished Iris and Faith wouldn't see him in this state. To his increasing embarrassment, the doctor began providing the two women an explicit summary of Hunter's condition. Hunter tried to protest, but his thoughts were too addled and his mouth was too dry to speak. The doctor used words like *muscle inflammation*, *steroids* and *neuropathy*. Although he couldn't make sense of everything the physician was saying, Hunter understood the gist of it to mean his condition was due to his original accident. His lack of ongoing physical therapy combined with muscle overuse had caused his condition to worsen progressively.

"Reaching over the seat like he did was the straw that broke the camel's back, so to speak," the doctor said. Then he emphasized, "*Not* that Hunter's back is broken—that's the good news. Sometimes when we see symptoms like these, it's because a broken bone is exerting pressure on the nerves. But his X-rays look great. And other than an egg-sized bump on the back of his skull, I don't think there's any reason to be concerned about his head injury, either."

"So he'll be able to walk again?" Faith's voice was quavering.

"Absolutely," the doctor asserted. "In fact, the trick will be to keep him from walking too far too soon. He needs to learn to pace himself."

After the doctor left, Hunter had to strain to hear Faith tell his mother, "I didn't know how badly he'd been hurt in the crash. I knew he lost his *daed*—your husband—in an accident, but I didn't realize Hunter sustained any permanent injuries."

My injuries are not *permanent!* Hunter felt like shouting.

"That's because he didn't want anyone to know," Iris confided. Hunter silently willed her to stop talking, but she continued. "My big, strong *suh*. He must have been in pain for so long, yet he never let on. I should have known. I'm his mother. I should have known my *kind* was in pain."

From the sound of his mother's sniffling, Hunter realized she was crying, and inwardly it made him cringe. Ordinarily, he might have regretted causing her such distress, but right now he only felt humiliated by her doting sentiments.

"It's not your fault, Iris," Faith argued. "If it's anyone's fault, it's mine. I asked him to make a second evening delivery. You heard what the doctor said about the straw that broke the camel's back. If it weren't for me—"

"Quiet!" Hunter finally managed to gasp. "You two are disrupting my sleep."

"Hunter, you're awake!" his mother declared,

and suddenly she was brushing his curls from his forehead.

"I am now." He grimaced, his eyes still shut. "It's hard to sleep with you two clucking over me like worried hens."

"I'm sorry," Faith apologized. "I can go back to the waiting room."

"*Gut* idea, and take my *mamm* with you," he said.

At least he that's what he thought he said; maybe he only imagined saying it, or perhaps it was a dream. When he woke, he could hear the patter of sleet against the window and what he guessed was his mother's rhythmic breathing as she slept in a chair nearby. He fluttered his eyelids open, trying to adjust to the faint fluorescent light.

"Can I get you something?" Faith whispered, quickly appearing at his side.

His mouth was too dry to speak, so he shook his head.

Faith lowered a bent straw to his lips so he could sip the water she offered.

"Are you in pain?" she asked, her mouth so close to his ear he could feel her warm breath on his cheek.

"*Neh,*" he answered falsely and shut his eyes so he wouldn't have to face her concerned, pitying expression.

When he woke again, it was morning and his hips were burning with pain. As he tried to adopt a more comfortable position, he was appalled to notice the lower half of his white, atrophied leg had been exposed from the knee down as he slept. Flipping the flimsy blanket over it, he moaned from the small exertion.

Startled awake, his mother sat upright. "Hunter, dear, how do you feel?" she asked.

"His mouth is probably dry. He might need a sip of water before he can answer," Faith suggested, rushing to his bed with a cup and straw.

"I'm fine. Stop talking about me like I'm not here," Hunter barked in a scratchy voice.

Both women looked taken aback, which irritated him all the more, but before he could say anything else, there was a rapid knock on the door.

"*Kumme* in," his mother called.

A new, younger doctor introduced himself and asked Hunter how he was feeling this morning.

"Fair," Hunter responded grimly.

"I'm surprised you're doing that well," the doctor commented, as he perused Hunter's chart. "But, with physical therapy, I have every confidence you'll regain your full strength. It's going to take time and you'll have to limit certain activities, especially riding in your buggy or sitting and standing for long periods. And it's vital that you continue the regimen until you've completed your course of PT."

After the doctor left, Hunter scoffed, "He only wants me to go to more physical therapy because that's how the *Englisch* clinicians make their money."

"Hunter," his mother argued, "if physical therapy keeps you from being bedridden again, it's worth every penny."

Hunter was mortified his mother disclosed he'd previously been confined to bed.

"I don't want to discuss this in front of *her*," he said, motioning toward Faith with a jerk of his thumb. "The last thing I need is all of Main Street knowing my private business, whether it's about my health or our finances."

Faith's face immediately blotched with color. "*Neh*, of course not. I promise not to say a word to anyone and I'll give you two your privacy now. My brothers will be here shortly to take me to the bakery. When they arrive, I'll have them stop in to make arrangements for bringing you both home once you're discharged, too, if that's alright?"

Hunter turned his face and closed his eyes, but his mother answered, "*Jah*, we would appreciate that. *Denki*, Faith, for everything you've done."

* * *

Wrapped in the fresh, dry shawl Lovina sent for her, Faith was quiet as she journeyed in Mason's buggy to Willow Creek. The temperature had risen, melting the ice, and the wet roads glittered in the morning sunshine. As they flew past the same landmarks Faith had felt as if she'd never reach the night before, she fretted over Hunter's parting words.

Understanding that pain could bring out the worst in people and recalling how miserable she'd been after her own surgery, Faith tried to dismiss his sentiment and tone. But it stung that he wouldn't even look at her or say her name. Perhaps Hunter decided she was responsible for his hospitalization. She couldn't blame him if he did. Despite Iris's insistence Faith wasn't at fault, Faith was having a difficult time letting go of her guilt. She shouldn't have asked him to travel to Marianne Palmer's house in inclement weather.

But how could she have known making deliveries would exact such a toll on his physical health? He never mentioned his previous injuries or indicated any kind of struggle. It was only in retrospect Faith realized the source of Hunter's awkward posture and somber expression: he was suffering.

The last thing Faith intended to do was add

to his hardship by giving information about his condition to anyone else. So, she made up her mind that when the *leit* asked her questions about his health—and they *would* ask, because they truly cared for each other—she'd refer them to him. She'd guard his secret as fiercely as if it were her own, and eventually he'd understand how trustworthy she was.

"It's out of the way, but could we stop at Ruth's?" Faith asked as they neared Main Street. "I'd like to update her and say hello to Henrietta before going to the bakery."

Mason waited in the buggy while Faith went inside, where the two women were sipping tea in the kitchen.

"Faith!" Henrietta exclaimed, flinging her arms around her sister-in-law. Faith hugged her back.

Then, with characteristic candor, Henrietta pulled away and said, "I hope Hunter is doing better than you are. You look exhausted."

"As soon as I have a cup of *kaffi*, I'll be wide awake. As for Hunter, I believe he'll be home this afternoon, so he can tell you himself how he feels. I stopped to see if there's anything either of you needs before I go to work."

"That was thoughtful," Henrietta remarked. "But we're as snug as can be. Don't tell Lovina this, since she's at home watching my *kinner* as well as her own, but once we were assured you and Hunter were alright, it was very peaceful spending the night here. I didn't anticipate how much I'll enjoy visiting you at your apartment when you move, Faith."

Ruth added, "*Jah*, but unlike me, Faith will have plenty of delicious treats on hand to offer you, such as apple fry pies. We've had to make do with sweet bread and honey."

Now that Hunter can't deliver my goodies to Piney Hill, I doubt I'll be moving into the apartment or even making delicious treats much longer, Faith thought. But she forced herself to smile. Before leaving, Faith told Henrietta she'd be home for supper, since Mason had brought her bicycle with them for her return trip.

Just as she expected, when she arrived at the bakery Pearl peppered Faith with questions about Hunter.

"Whatever happened to our dear boy?" she asked before Faith crossed the threshold of the back entrance. "I knew something was wrong, but when I asked him he told me he was fine. What did the doctors say is the matter with him?"

Again, Faith felt overwhelmed by guilt. If she hadn't been so preoccupied with her own financial worries, might she have noticed Hunter was in no condition to go to the Palmers' house?

"I don't know the correct terms for his condition, Pearl," Faith answered truthfully. "But when he's out of the hospital, you can ask him. Meanwhile, Ruth said the cannery should remain closed."

At that, Ivy emerged from the storefront. "Hunter Schwartz is in the hospital. The cannery sign says Closed. I will work here until the cannery sign says Open," she stated definitively.

Pearl raised an eyebrow at Faith. "It would allow one of us to dedicate ourselves to baking," the older woman suggested.

It would also cost Faith more money in salaries. But now that she likely wasn't going to meet her financial goal anyway, what did it really matter if she paid Ivy for a few extra hours? Faith knew Ivy would be at a loss without a daily routine to follow, just like she was the week the cannery was closed after Ruth's fall. Besides, Ivy provided a beneficial service to holiday shoppers: with her help in the storefront, the line would continue to move quickly.

"We'd welcome your help until Hunter reopens the cannery, Ivy," Faith said. "But no more baking for you—I don't want you to burn yourself again. And it's very important you don't tell customers or anyone else that Hunter went to the hospital."

"No more baking," Ivy agreed, before returning to the storefront. "And I won't tell anyone Hunter Schwartz went to the hospital."

"As for you and me," Faith said to Pearl, "how about if I focus on filling orders, if you don't mind managing the register for Ivy?"

"Of course. When it's slow, I'll give you a hand in the back."

"*Neh*, when it's slow, you can take a break. You deserve one. I'll keep up with the orders the best as I can, but if we have to turn some away, then we'll do that. It's not worth...not worth an accident or any tension between us, Pearl," Faith replied, her voice warbling.

Pearl waved her hand, saying, "It's okay."

"*Neh*, it's not okay. My behavior to you recently has been unacceptable. You're not just an employee here, you're my friend and I'm very sorry I acted so demanding after everything you've done to support me."

"It's okay," Pearl repeated. "I understand why you've been so tense. I'm sorry, too, for carrying on as I did. Sometimes I can be a bit stuck in my ways."

"*Neh*, you were right. The gingerbread men *are* crunchier than the round cookies and they break far too easily." Remembering how Hunter joked about landing on the box of gingerbread men in the backseat of the buggy, and imagining his pain, Faith burst into tears.

Pearl handed her a handkerchief and then patted her back. "There, there. You must have had a terrible fright. But Hunter's alright now. You'll see. Everything's going to be just fine."

Everything was going to be just fine? Knowing what she did about Hunter's injuries, the last words he'd spoken to her, the status of their deliveries and the uncertainty of her future, Faith thought Pearl's words sounded like a hollow promise, but she lifted her head and dried her tears.

"Enough of my sniveling," she announced. "I should get to work—but first I think I'll have a cream-filled doughnut. I'm famished."

"I don't need your help," Hunter snapped. "I need my privacy."

The nurse scowled but said nothing. Hunter knew she probably thought because he was an Amish man, he was too modest to have a female nurse help him with his morning routine, and it was true, he was. But it was more than mere modesty that kept him from accepting her assistance—it was independence. He didn't need help with his clothes, nor did he need to drink from a straw, like a baby from a bottle. What he needed was to have the room to himself so he could get ready to go home.

However, once the nurse vacated the room,

Hunter became heady as he tried to stand. He sat back down and waited for the room to stop spinning so he could put on the clean clothes Mason Yoder had brought him. Unable to bend at his waist, he decided to forgo wearing socks altogether. But as he attempted to wiggle his foot into his boot, his lower back was seized by a cramp that was so excruciating he stumbled forward. The male nurse, Tyler, burst through the door and caught him just in time. He assisted Hunter with his socks as well as his boots, and then briefly left, returning a minute later with a wheelchair and a cane.

"This is your new best friend for the next several weeks," he quipped, displaying the dark wooden stick with rubber padding on the handle and tip. "You'll need to lean on it whenever you walk. Unless, of course, you're out with your girlfriend, in which case, you've got the perfect excuse to hold her hand."

It annoyed Hunter how brazen the *Englisch* were about discussing personal relationships. "I don't have a girlfriend," he snapped. *And if I ever had a chance of courting Faith, it's gone now.*

"Faith isn't your girlfriend? Oh, man, that's too bad," Tyler replied, shaking his head. "She was so concerned about you I assumed you two were a couple. Anyway, here you go, it's all yours."

When Tyler pushed the stick toward him, Hunter shook his head and muttered, "Canes are for old men."

Tyler shrugged. "It's up to you if you take it or not. But I guarantee if you don't, you're going to fall and end up more miserable than you are right now."

Hunter eyed the young, brawny *Englisch* man who appeared to be the picture of health. "What would you know about falling?" he challenged. "Or about being miserable?"

"Plenty. I broke my leg in a motorcycle accident when I was eighteen," Tyler said. "But I was like you—too stubborn for my own good. Afterward, I refused to use a cane and one day I wiped out on a crack in a concrete sidewalk. A sidewalk! I ended up in traction."

Glowering, Hunter snatched the cane from Tyler's outstretched hand. Leveraging his weight against it, he transitioned from the bed to the wheelchair, and then the nurse wheeled him to the front entrance while his mother followed behind.

"What's this?" Hunter asked when a taxi pulled to the curb in front of them. "Where's our buggy? Faith brought me here in our buggy."

"One of the Yoder brothers took it home for

us. The weather was bad overnight and the horse needed to be fed and sheltered. The hospital arranged for your transportation home because they wanted you to be comfortable. It's all paid for, too," his mother explained. "Wasn't that generous?"

"We don't need charity from the *Englisch*," Hunter snapped. "It's bad enough we have to take it from the Amish *leit*."

As if apologizing for a temperamental child's behavior, Hunter's mother whispered to Tyler, "I'm so sorry. I don't know what's gotten into him."

"I do," Tyler said, directing his encouragement at Hunter. "But it will pass, trust me."

Ignoring him, Hunter used the arms of the wheelchair to push himself into a standing position. "Ach!" he hollered in anguish and frustration as he teetered.

Tyler dived forward to steady him. "Remember your new best friend," he reproached, placing the cane across Hunter's knees once he was safely situated in the backseat. "You need to lean on this everywhere you go. Unless you wise up and ask a pretty redhead to hold your hand."

Tyler closed the door and then he escorted Hunter's mother to the other side of the vehicle, and Iris slid into the seat next to her son.

Because traveling by car made his mother nervous, Hunter usually tried to distract her with small talk, but today he was too physically and emotionally depleted to do anything other than stare out the window.

As they sped along the Pennsylvania countryside, Hunter was reminded of the van trip that brought them to Willow Creek a month ago. Suddenly he realized he was back to square one in regard to his finances—and maybe he was even worse off than before he began working for Faith. His earnings from the deliveries wouldn't cover the cost of his hospital stay, and he was more annoyed than comforted by his suspicion Ruth would insist on contributing to his bills. Hunter had journeyed to Willow Creek specifically to assist her; instead, he was becoming a burden. Not only was he failing to keep his aunt's cannery running smoothly, but he was failing to support himself and his mother, and he was failing to help Faith support herself, too. If he didn't get back on his feet again soon and accomplish what he'd set out to do, those failures would be more painful to him than his injuries ever were.

Chapter Ten

By Saturday afternoon, Faith was worried. She hadn't heard a word about Hunter's condition since she'd left the hospital. She stopped in at Schrock's Shop on Friday because she knew Joseph had gone to see Hunter on Thursday, but all Joseph said was Hunter was asleep when he visited. Torn between wanting to respect Hunter's privacy and wanting to offer support, Faith decided she'd wait until Monday, and if she hadn't heard anything by then, she'd visit Ruth's household with some treats.

Saturday evening was the first opportunity she had to examine her bookkeeping to assess whether she could still meet her financial goal. After putting the supper dishes away, she opened her ledger at the kitchen table. Hunter had organized her accounts so fastidiously that Faith had no trouble working out the figures now. She marveled that she'd actually profited more in the past several weeks than in the previous several months combined. However, she estimated she was still at least $600 short of making the down payment on the lease. She calculated she could net up to $250 before the year's end, but even that would be a stretch, especially now that she wasn't baking for the festival and she had Ivy's full-time salary to pay.

Faith crossed her arms on top of the paperwork and buried her head in them. The future she planned was gone. It was time for her to give up. She had to accept that owning a business apparently wasn't God's will for her.

"Faith?" Henrietta asked. Faith hadn't heard her come in. "What's wrong?"

"I can't do it." She sniffed and raised her head. "I can't make the lease down payment. I have until January 1 to close the bakery, move my things out and tell Pearl she doesn't have a job anymore."

"But you've literally worn yourself to the bone trying to accomplish your goal. Look at your dress," Henrietta said, pinching the excess fabric where it hung loosely around Faith's waist. "You've worked too hard to lose your business."

"Apparently, I didn't work hard enough."

"Sometimes, hard work isn't what you need—

what you need is graciousness." Henrietta announced, "That's why Noah and I decided we want to give you a loan of up to five hundred dollars."

"What?" Faith was incredulous. "But I thought you didn't want me to move away from the farm!"

"I don't," admitted Henrietta. "Because I'll miss you. Don't you know that? I have a special bond with you that I don't share with anyone else, not with Lovina, not even with Willa. But I can't allow my selfish desires to interfere with *Gott's* plan for your life."

Touched by her sister-in-law's generosity, Faith swallowed, suppressing a sob. "Henrietta, I don't know what to say."

"Say you'll accept the loan. And promise me I'll be the first person you have over for tea."

"I promise." Faith giggled, throwing her arms around her sister-in-law's shoulders. "Just don't tell Andy—he thinks he's coming over for peanut butter sheet cake the first day I move in."

As she lay in bed that night, Faith imagined how euphoric Pearl would be to hear about the loan. Ivy would be glad, as well. But the person Faith was most eager to tell was Hunter. Were it not for his partnership, she never would have come so close to meeting her goal. She fell asleep picturing his smile when she told him the great news.

The next morning she woke to her nephews' jubilant cheers: overnight Willow Creek had been transformed by a glittering snowfall. The little boys' wonderment and the scintillating landscape enhanced Faith's joy about the loan and her anticipation about seeing Hunter again.

"*Ant* Faith," Andy beckoned. "*Daed* said he'd take us sledding by Wheeler's Bridge. Will you *kumme*, too?"

Faith couldn't resist. "*Jah*, of course. I'll ask your *daed* if we can stop to see if the Miller *kinner* want to join us, too. I brought something home from the bakery I was planning to give them anyway."

Isaac Miller was delighted to accept the two loaves of bread and jar of preserves Faith brought him by way of apology, and his children were even happier to join Faith's nephews sledding on the big hill.

"I'll stand at the bottom to make sure the *kinner* don't veer toward the pond," Reuben informed her. "The surface is frozen, but with the snow cover, I can't assess how thick the ice is underneath. I wouldn't want them to fall through."

Faith remained at the top of the hill, aligning the children on their sleds before giving them running pushes. She whooped and clapped as they careened down the long, gradual descent, shrieking and shouting all the way to the bottom.

"I don't know who's having more fun, you or the *kinner*," a soft voice said behind her.

"Iris, hello!" Faith trilled. "I've been thinking of you and Ruth, and praying for Hunter. How is he?"

"He's doing better physically," Iris said. "But I'm afraid his mood is no better than what you experienced at the hospital."

Faith loosened her scarf around her mouth. "I was in the hospital once," she confided. "And for about a week after I was discharged, I was so dismal I think everyone in my family wanted to send me back."

Iris laughed. "*Jah*, I figured since I couldn't tell him to go take a walk, I'd take one myself."

"May I visit him?" Faith asked. "I have news that might cheer him up."

Iris's face clouded over. "I don't know if that would be a *gut* idea right now," she said.

Faith didn't wish to exacerbate Iris's stress. "I understand. How about if I send a quick note? Henrietta keeps a pen and paper in the buggy. I'll walk back that way with you."

Faith signaled Reuben at the bottom of the hill, where the children were lobbing snowballs at him. "I'll be right back," she called. He gave her a thumbs-up signal before scooping a heap of snow to toss in the children's direction.

Iris smiled. "Hunter always enjoyed his exploits with your brothers when he was little. He'd come home and announce that when he became a *daed*, he was going to have at least six *kinner*. He thought it was great the Yoder boys had so many brothers."

Ignoring the barb of resentment she felt whenever the subject of large families came up, Faith drolly replied, "Spoken like someone who never had to wait his turn for the washroom."

"Or keep the floors clean with six boys tromping through the house!" Iris declared, and the two women didn't stop laughing until they reached the buggy.

Hunter, Faith wrote on a small square of paper she ripped from the bottom of Henrietta's grocery list, *I pray you are doing better each day. I look forward to seeing you when you're ready for company. Meanwhile, I have exciting news I couldn't wait to share: Reuben and Henrietta are providing me a loan—I get to keep the bakery!* Deciding she couldn't adequately express her appreciation for Hunter's help on the tiny scrap of paper, Faith concluded by simply signing her name. She'd thank him in person later.

As she watched Iris trudge through the snow to Ruth's house, it occurred to Faith that Hunter's mother probably wanted to have more children as much as Hunter wanted to have a sibling. *We don't always get what we want*, Faith reminded herself, just as she'd done the morning she hired Hunter. Back then, what she desired more than anything was to keep her bakery. And now, because of God's abundant blessing, through hard work and help from Pearl, Hunter and her family, Faith's business was secure. She had gotten exactly what she wanted, and she was grateful.

So then, what was this yearning still gnawing at her heart? And why, as she plodded back toward the children, did she suddenly feel more like weeping than laughing?

Because the snowfall made the ground especially slippery, Hunter secluded himself in his room for most of Sunday afternoon. He was practicing walking without a cane when Ruth called to him, so he picked up the stick again and toddled into the parlor.

Back from her stroll, his mother was warming her hands by the stove. "There's something your *ant* and I want to discuss with you," she said. "Do you need help sitting down?"

"*Neh*, I can manage." Hunter eased his body

onto the sofa with the aid of his cane. "I've grown accustomed to using this stick. I think if I stand on a milking stool, I can maneuver myself into the buggy, so I should be able to go to town tomorrow to reopen the cannery."

"That's what I want to discuss," Ruth replied. "To be candid, I've decided not to renew the lease on the cannery next year, and since you're still recovering and we haven't continued to put up jars for the holiday season, there's no sense reopening the shop. Instead, I'll talk to Faith about stocking a few items on a shelf in her bakery. Now that her business is booming, I anticipate she'll be glad to keep Ivy on permanently, provided she's able to make her down payment."

If Hunter hadn't already been seated, the magnitude of his aunt's announcement would have knocked him flat. "I don't understand. You've run the cannery for years."

"*Jah*, but the doctor told me it's time to slow down. While I'm not ready to be put out to pasture quite yet, I do have other undertakings I'd like to focus on at home and in our community."

Hunter narrowed his eyes. It wasn't like Ruth to take an *Englischer's* advice, even if he was a doctor. Why hadn't she consulted Hunter about the decision? Then he realized *he* was the reason she was closing shop. She probably thought he'd fallen so far behind on the sales it wasn't worth the effort to catch up. "I'm sorry, *Ant* Ruth. I know I've disappointed you," Hunter apologized. "But if you give me another chance—"

Ruth cut him off. "How have you disappointed me? By injuring yourself because you were working so hard? If I had compensated you, as I should have insisted on doing, you never would have taken a second job," she railed. "*You* disappointed *me*? Ha! You've seen my books. You know the business is doing fine. You, however, are *not* doing fine. Anyone can see that."

"*Neh*, really, I'm—"

"Hush up and listen to your old *ant*, because there's something else I need to tell you," she warned, pointing a finger at Hunter. "Since I already set aside the down payment for next year's lease, I want you and your *mamm* to have it. It will cover any outstanding bills you have in Parkersville, and it should help with your physical therapy costs, too."

Hunter grimaced and adjusted his posture. "*Denki*, that's very generous of you, *Ant* Ruth, but it isn't necessary."

Before his aunt could reply, Iris firmly stated, "*Suh*, I believe it *is* necessary. I appreciate that you've tried to protect me from worrying about our mortgage payments, but I'm aware the bills must be stacking up. Ruth and I discussed the matter earlier and I believe we should gratefully accept her gift to us. As far as the cannery goes, it's up to Ruth to determine what to do with her business, and I know you'll respect whatever she decides."

Hunter's shoulders stiffened and he clamped his jaw shut. So, the two of them had made up their minds without so much as considering his opinion first. He felt so disregarded he could hardly look at them. "I should tend to the animals," he said flatly.

"Ach! I forgot," his mother remarked as he was pulling himself to his feet. "I saw Faith by Wheeler's Bridge when I went for my walk. She asked me to give you this." She handed him a folded square of paper.

Faith. Of course! She probably wanted to know when he could resume making deliveries. As Hunter shambled toward the stable, he was struck with a plan. The doctor didn't *prohibit* him from riding in the buggy; he just advised him to limit the length of his journeys. Hunter figured without the cannery to manage, he could take his time running Faith's deliveries, stopping to stretch his muscles along the way. Perhaps he could even make a few additional deliveries to local customers.

As he hobbled toward the stable, Hunter's mood brightened. There was still a way to help Faith meet her goal. There was still time to prove that Ruth's gift wasn't necessary, and that Hunter could take care of his mother, just as his father trusted him to do. And there was still hope that maybe he'd be able to support a wife and family of his own one day, too.

When he reached the outer building, Hunter unfolded the piece of paper. The dusky light glowed enough for him to read Faith's message. After his behavior in the hospital, Hunter wouldn't have been surprised if she wanted to keep her distance, so he smiled to read she was eager to see him again. But his optimism plummeted with her words; *Reuben and Henrietta are providing me a loan.* Apparently, his services were no longer required.

First his aunt and mother, and now Faith had lost confidence in his abilities. Even though he hadn't given up on helping them, they'd given up on him. And why wouldn't they? He disappointed them when they needed him most. He felt so hurt, angry and ashamed that he whacked his cane against a post—once, twice, three times before it split in half—rendering it just as broken and useless as he was.

Although Faith didn't receive a visit from Hunter on Monday as she had hoped, early Tuesday morning, she heard someone drumming the back door. "Hunter!" she exclaimed as she unbolted the lock.

"*Neh*, it's me, Joseph Schrock."

Faith wiped the back of her hand against her brow to conceal her embarrassment. "*Guder mariye*, Joseph. Please *kumme* in. I'll pour you a cup of *kaffi*."

"*Denki*, but I can't stay. I came to town early this morning to prepare for the rush of *Englisch* holiday shoppers. Last night Amity and I paid a visit to Ruth Graber's household, and I was asked to give you this."

Faith was so eager to read the note Joseph presented her she didn't even inquire about Hunter's condition. When Joseph departed, she tore open the envelope.

Dear Faith, the message read. Faith recognized the flowery penmanship as Ruth's, and her smile wilted; she'd assumed the note was from Hunter. *I have something important concerning the cannery I'd like to speak with you about. If you could call on me at your convenience, I'd appreciate it.* Ruth ended the note by asking Faith to extend her greetings to Pearl, Ivy, and Faith's family.

What could Ruth have to tell her about the cannery? Faith wondered if the news was related to Hunter's injuries, and she fretted his condition had worsened. Perhaps that was why he hadn't responded to Faith's note? Now that Ruth invited her to stop by, Faith wouldn't have to wait any longer to find out how Hunter was faring. If only she had known she'd be visiting, Faith would have brought from home the small "get well and thank you" gift she'd gotten for him: a reflective vest to keep him safe on his early morning walks as he recovered.

Shortly before one o'clock, Faith told Pearl and Ivy she wouldn't be dining with them during their break.

"If you're working through dinner, so will I," Pearl offered.

"*Neh*, I'm not working—I'm riding my bicycle to Ruth's house. She loves my apple fry pies and I want to deliver some while they're still warm."

Pearls lips curled. "He—I mean *she* will appreciate them. Please give my *gut* wishes to Hunter while you're there, too. Don't hurry back. We'll take care of everything here, won't we, Ivy?"

"*Jah*, we'll turn the sign to Open at one thirty," Ivy agreed, "so Faith Yoder can visit Hunter Schwartz at Ruth Graber's house."

Faith laughed; although she'd been summoned to Ruth's house by Ruth herself, there was no sense denying that seeing Hunter was her ulterior motive for taking a midday jaunt.

"Oh, Faith, you know those are my favorite!" Ruth applauded when she discovered Faith brought apple fry pies. "Iris will put a kettle on while you warm yourself by the stove. Your cheeks are bright—it must be very cold out there."

"*Jah*, it's freezing," Faith admitted, glancing toward the hallway. If Hunter was in the house, she couldn't hear him.

While Iris was fixing a tray, Faith inquired after Ruth's health. It was then Ruth disclosed she didn't intend to reopen the cannery. Faith readily agreed to sell certain remaining jarred goods in her bakery, and she was delighted to accept Ivy as a permanent employee.

"I want you to do what's best for your well-being, Ruth, but our dinner breaks won't be the same without you," Faith lamented.

"Oh, you won't be rid of me—I plan to join you fine women for dinner as often as possible," Ruth promised as she handed Faith the key to the cannery and a list of goods to sell.

"Has Hunter tried your apple fry pies?" Iris questioned when she returned with a tray of teacups. "He loves your baking."

"Why don't you beckon him?" Ruth suggested. "I believe he's out by the stable."

"Of course." Faith grinned and donned her shawl, scarf and gloves.

She approached the building just as Hunter tottered out of it, balancing against what looked like a walking stick whittled from a tree limb. She didn't know if he was scowling from pain or merely squinting against the sunlight, but she was so tickled to see him she rushed in his direction.

"*Guder nammidaag*, Hunter," she said. "It's *wunderbaar* to see you out and about!"

"Were you expecting me to be bedridden?" he asked. There was a hardness about his mouth and jaw that indicated he wasn't jesting.

"*Neh*. I only meant I'm happy to see you. I've been praying for you and wondering how you're feeling."

Hunter frowned. "What are you doing here in the middle of the day?" he asked without addressing her concern.

"Ruth needed to talk to me, and I wanted to bring her some apple fry pies. We're about to have them with tea."

"You'd better get back inside, then."

Although his dismissal hurt, Faith thought perhaps she hadn't made it clear he was invited, too. "Would you like to join us?" she asked.

"*Neh,*" was his succinct reply.

Faith felt buffaloed by his bluntness. Was he upset with her? Was that why he wasn't conversing or acknowledging the big news in her note? After working so hard to help her accomplish her goal, Faith thought Hunter would have been pleased she was getting a loan. Did he feel slighted that she hadn't expressed more appreciation?

"Alright, but I can't leave without saying *denki* for all your help recently. I don't know what I would have done without—"

Hunter didn't allow her to complete her sentiment. "Running deliveries was my job and you already paid me for my service. There's no need to say *denki* again."

Faith's mouth dropped open. He was making it clear he no longer considered her to be a friend; he considered her to be an employer—a former employer, at that. Maybe even a stranger, given the distant look in his eyes. Faith was crushed. "Oh, okay, then," she uttered. "*Mach's gut*, Hunter."

She swiveled toward the house and was halfway across the yard when she dashed back to where he loitered at the threshold of the stable. Like the bakery, their relationship meant too much to Faith to let it go without doing everything she could to save it.

Peering into his dark, impassive eyes, Faith implored, "I'm so sorry I pushed you to make a second trip to the Palmers' house during the ice storm. If you hadn't helped me with that last-minute delivery, you wouldn't have strained your back. I don't blame you for being angry with me. If you'll let me, I'll do anything I can to help you as you recover. I just hope in time you'll forgive me."

Hunter's expression remained as unyielding as the frozen ground beneath their feet. "I understand the bakery is the center of your life, Faith, but neither you nor it is responsible for my injuries, so there's nothing for me to forgive. As for my recovery, I don't need or want your help."

His caustic remarks made Faith's eyes smart, but she managed to hold back her tears. She suspected Hunter's indifference and self-sufficiency were a facade to conceal how wounded he felt. She should know; she had often acted that way herself. Perhaps by inviting Hunter into her secret sorrow, she could draw him out of his.

"I appreciate that struggling with a health issue can be a lonely, frightening experience," she began.

"What would you know about my struggles?" Hunter jeered, balancing his weight to thrust his walking stick under Faith's nose. "What would you know about walking down the street using one of these? Or about losing your job because you can't move half as fast as you used to?"

Although he noticed Faith's face blanch and

her eyes fill, Hunter couldn't seem to stop himself from haranguing her. "How often do you lie in bed counting every second until your muscle spasms subside? Did you ever hesitate to hold a *bobbel* because you're afraid your back might seize up and you'll drop him? And speaking of *bobblin*, when was the last time someone laced your boots for you, as if you were a pitiful little *kind*?"

Faith wiped a tear from her cheek. "I am so sorry that you've been—that you *are*—suffering. It's true, I don't know what your pain feels like. But I do know what it feels like to have a body that isn't capable…that isn't exactly as I wish it would be."

"Ha!" Hunter roared, glaring down at her. "Being a couple of pounds overweight isn't anything like having chronic back, hip and leg pain. All you have to do is go on a diet for a few days. I have months, maybe years, of physical therapy to endure. Expenses aside, do you have any idea how exacting that's going to be? So don't you dare whine about your weight to me!"

Faith gasped, momentarily recoiling. Then she thrust her hands onto her hips, stepped forward and bore into him with her eyes as she retorted, "For your information, I wasn't referring to my weight, but *denki* for pointing out I should go on a diet. I'll start by forgoing the apple fry pies I brought. Please tell your *ant* and your *mamm* I'm sorry I had to leave, but something ruined my appetite."

Agape, Hunter watched Faith storm to where she'd leaned her bicycle against a tree. Before getting on, she whirled around and shouted, "If you want people to stop treating you like a pitiful little *kind*, then you ought to start acting like a man, Hunter Schwartz!"

Hunter was so peeved he might have broken his walking stick just as he'd broken his cane if he hadn't caught a glimpse of his mother in the picture window. The two women inside undoubtedly watched—and possibly heard—his altercation with Faith as it unfolded, and they were probably shaking their heads about it now. He didn't care. His words may have seemed unkind but they weren't untrue, and it was a relief to have admitted how he felt.

He pulled open the door to the stable and went inside where they couldn't see him walking without his stick. Navigating the interior from post to post, he seethed over Faith's departing comment. She might as well have kicked him in the shins for the blow she delivered to his manhood by telling him he was acting like a *kind*. After all he'd done to disguise his pain so he could help her with deliveries! If there was any consolation in Ruth shutting down the cannery, it was that Hunter wouldn't have to return to Main Street. *I don't care if I never see Faith again*, he thought. *I can't return to Indiana soon enough.*

Around and around he paced until his fuming was interrupted by his mother's voice. "Hunter?" she said from the entryway. "You must be deep in thought—you didn't hear me calling your name."

"Oh," he said noncommittally. He hoped she wasn't going to press him for information about what transpired between Faith and him.

Instead, she perched on a bale of hay, hugged her shawl tightly around her and said, "There's something I wanted to say the other day, but not in front of Ruth. Could you please stop your marching and *kumme* sit for a moment?" His mother patted the hay.

Hunter hadn't realized he was still moving. He gingerly lowered himself into a sitting position on the bale of hay. "What is it you'd like to discuss?" he asked.

"Living here with your *ant* has been a blessing to me. Caring for her has helped me stop focusing on my grief over losing your *daed*. I won't ever stop missing him, but I clearly see now that the Lord still has work for me to do. I believe part of that work is to care for Ruth in her later years. It's what she needs, and it helps ease my loneliness, too."

Hunter gulped, fearing his mother wished to extend their stay in Willow Creek.

"I think you and I are opposites," she said. "You're more like your *daed*. You need to learn to rely more on other people and I need to learn to stop relying on them so much. I've leaned heavily on you since your *daed* died, and it's time I stand on my own two feet again—with more of *Gott's* help and less of yours."

"Neh," Hunter contradicted. "You haven't leaned too hard on me, *Mamm.*"

"Jah, I have. And I couldn't have made it to this point without your help, so I'm very grateful. But you're a young man. You should be thinking about a wife, not about supporting your *mamm.* I know you'll always care for me and help me wherever you are, Hunter. It's what kind of *suh* you are. But I've decided I'm not going back to live in Indiana. There are too many memories of your *daed* there, and Ruth needs me here. I think you should consider selling the house. I know we won't make much of a profit, but whatever we make, half of it is yours to do with what you choose. If you want to return to Parkersville permanently, you may. If you'd prefer to stay in Willow Creek, Ruth has already said you are *wilkom* to live with us."

"But *Mamm*—"

His mother squeezed his hand with her gloved fingers. "*But* nothing. The only thing worse than being in pain myself is watching my *kind* suffer. You didn't have a choice about whether you suffered physical pain from the accident. But you do have a choice about whether you continue to suffer unnecessary emotional pain. It's up to you."

"What do you mean?"

"I think you know, *suh*," she replied. "I've witnessed how deeply you and Faith cherish each other."

Even in the frigid air, Hunter's ears burned. He opened his mouth to tell his mother she couldn't be more mistaken, but the words that came out were, "I'm… I'm hungry. Are there any apple fry pies left?"